Fairest

The Lunar Chronicles

Levana's Story

WRITTEN BY

Marissa Meyer

A FEIWEL AND FRIENDS BOOK
An Imprint of Macmillan

Library of Congress Cataloging-in-Publication Data

Meyer, Marissa.
Fairest / Marissa Meyer. — First edition.
pages cm. — (Lunar chronicles ; book 4)
Summary: "Queen Levana is a ruler who uses her 'glamour' to gain power.
But long before she crossed paths with Cinder, Scarlet, and Cress,
Levana lived a very different story—a story that has never been
told . . . until now" — Provided by publisher.
[1. Science fiction.   2. Kings, queens, rulers, etc.—Fiction.
3. Cyborgs—Fiction.   4. Extraterrestrial beings—Fiction.]   I. Title.
PZ7.M571737 Fai 2015
[Fic]—dc23
2014042420

ISBN
978-1-250-06055-6 (hardcover)
978-1-250-06959-7 (Target edition)
978-1-250-06966-5 (international edition)
978-1-250-06874-3 (ebook)

Feiwel and Friends logo designed by Filomena Tuosto

First Edition: 2015

10 9 8 7 6 5

macteenbooks.com

This book is for the readers.
The Lunartics. The fans.
Thank you for taking this journey with me.

Mirror, mirror, on the wall.

Who is the Fairest of them all?

SHE WAS LYING ON A BURNING PYRE, HOT COALS BENEATH her back. White sparks floated in her vision but the mercy of unconsciousness wouldn't come. Her throat was hoarse from screaming. The smell of her own burning flesh invaded her nostrils. Smoke stung her eyes. Blisters burbled across her skin, and entire swaths of flesh peeled away, revealing raw tissue underneath.

The pain was relentless, the agony never ending. She pleaded for death, but it never came.

She reached out with her good hand, trying to drag her body from the fire, but the bed of coals crushed and collapsed under her weight, burying her, dragging her deeper into the embers and the smoke.

Through the haze she caught a glimpse of kind eyes. A warm smile. A finger curled toward her. *Come here, baby sister . . .*

Levana gasped and jolted upward, limbs tangled in heavy blankets. Her sheets were damp and cold from her sweat, but her skin was still burning hot from the dream. Her throat felt scratched raw. She struggled to swallow, but her saliva tasted like smoke and made her cringe. She sat in the faint morning light shuddering, trying to will away the nightmare. The same nightmare that had plagued her for too many years, that she could never seem to escape.

She rubbed her hands repeatedly over her arms and sides until she was certain the fire wasn't real. She was not burning alive. She was safe and alone in her chambers.

With a trembling breath, she scooted to the other side of the mattress, away from the sweat-stained sheets, and lay back down. Afraid to close her eyes, she stared up at the canopy and practiced her slow breathing until her heartbeat steadied.

She tried to distract herself by planning who she would be that day.

A thousand possibilities floated before her. She would be beautiful, but there were many types of beauty. Skin tone, hair texture, the shape of one's eyes, the length of a neck, a well-placed freckle, a certain grace in the way one walked.

Levana knew a great deal about beauty, just as she knew a great deal about ugliness.

Then she remembered that today was the funeral.

She groaned at the thought. How exhausting it would be to hold a glamour all day long, in front of so many. She didn't want to go, but she would have no choice.

It was an inconvenient day for her focus to be shaken by nightmares. Perhaps it would be best to choose something familiar.

As the dream receded into her subconscious, Levana toyed with the idea of being her mother that day. Not as Queen Jannali had been when she died, but perhaps as a fifteen-year-old version of her. It would be a sort of homage to attend the funeral wearing her mother's cheekbones and the vivid violet eyes that everyone knew were glamour-made, though no one would have dared say so aloud.

She spent a few minutes imagining what her mother might have looked like at her age, and she let the glamour settle over her. Moon-blonde hair sleekly pulled into a low knot. Skin as pale as a sheet of ice. A little shorter than she would become full grown. Pale pink lips, so as not to detract from the vibrancy of those eyes.

It calmed her, sinking into the glamour. But no sooner had she tested the look than she felt the wrongness of it.

She did not want to go to her parents' funeral in the garb of a girl-now-dead.

A tap fluttered at the door, interrupting her thoughts.

Levana sighed, and quickly fell into another costume that she'd dreamed up days before. Olive skin, a graceful slope to her nose, and raven-black hair cut adorably short. She shifted through a few eye colors before landing on a striking gray-blue, topped off with smoldering black lashes.

Before she could second-guess herself, she embedded a silver jewel into the flesh beneath her right eye.

A teardrop. To prove that she was in mourning.

"Come in," she called, opening her eyes.

A servant entered carrying a breakfast tray. The girl curtsied in the doorway, not lifting her gaze from the floor—which rendered Levana's glamour unnecessary—before approaching the bed.

"Good morning, Your Highness."

Sitting up, Levana allowed the servant to set the tray across her lap and tuck a cloth napkin around her. The servant poured jasmine tea into a hand-painted porcelain cup that had been imported from Earth several generations ago, and garnished it with two small mint leaves and a drizzle of honey. Levana said nothing as the servant uncovered a tray of tiny cream-filled pastries, so that Levana could see what they looked like whole, before using a silver knife to saw them into even tinier bite-size pieces. While the servant worked, Levana eyed the dish of bright-colored fruits: a soft-fuzzed peach set into a halo of black and red berries, all dusted with powdered sugar.

"Is there anything else I can bring for you, Your Highness?"

"No, that will be all. But send the other one up in twenty minutes to prepare my mourning dress."

"Of course, Your Highness," she answered, although they both knew there was no *other one*. Every servant in the palace was *the other one*. It didn't matter to Levana who the girl sent up, so long as whoever it was could properly stitch her into the sleek gray gown the seamstress had delivered the day before. Levana didn't want to bother with glamouring her dress today in addition to her face, not with so many other thoughts in her head.

With another curtsy, the servant ducked out of the room, leaving Levana to stare down at her breakfast tray. Only now did she realize how very un-hungry she was. There was an ache in her stomach, perhaps left over from the horrible dream. Or she supposed it could have been sadness, but that was doubtful.

She felt no great loss at the death of her parents, who had been gone now for half the long day. Eight artificial nights. Their deaths were terribly gory. They were assassinated by a shell who used his invincibility against the Lunar gift to sneak into the palace. The man had shot two royal guards in the head before making his way to her parents' bedroom on the third floor, killing three more guards, and slitting her mother's throat so deeply the knife severed part of her spine. He had then gone down the hallway to where her father was lying with one of his mistresses and stabbed him sixteen times in the chest.

The mistress was still screaming, blood spurts across her face, when two royal guards found them.

The shell murderer was still stabbing.

Levana had not seen the bodies, but she had seen the bedrooms the next morning, and her first thought was that all that blood would make for a very pretty rouge on her lips.

She knew it was not the proper thing to think, but she also did not think her parents would have thought anything better had it been *her* murdered instead of them.

Levana had managed to eat three-quarters of a pastry and five small berries when her bedroom door opened again. She was immediately angry at the intrusion—the servant was early. Only on the heels of her annoyance did she check that her glamour was still in place. This, she knew, was the wrong order of concern.

But it was her sister, not one of the faceless servants, who swept into her bedroom. "Channary!" Levana barked, pushing the tray away from her. The tea slopped over the sides of the cup, pooling in the saucer beneath. "I have not given you permission to enter."

"Then perhaps you should lock your door," said Channary, sliding like an eel across the carpet. "There are murderers about, you know."

She said it with a smile, wholly unconcerned. And why shouldn't she be? The murderer had been promptly executed when the guards found him, bloodied knife still in hand.

Not that Levana didn't think there could be more shells out there, angry enough and crazy enough to attempt another attack. Channary was a fool if she thought otherwise.

Which was part of the problem. Channary was simply a fool.

She was a beautiful fool, though, which was the worst kind. Her sister had lovely tanned skin and dark chestnut hair and eyes that tilted up just right at the corners so that she looked like she was smiling even when she wasn't. Levana was convinced that her sister's beauty was glamour-made, certain that no one as horrible on the inside could be so lovely on the outside, but Channary would never confess one way or the other. If there was a chink in her illusion of beauty, Levana had yet to find it. The stupid girl wasn't even bothered by mirrors.

Channary was already dressed for the funeral, though

the dull gray color of the fabric was the only indication that it was made for mourning. The netted skirt jutted out nearly perpendicular to her thighs, like a dancer's costume, and the body-hugging top was inset with thousands of silver sparkles. Her arms were painted with wide gray stripes spiraling up each limb, then coming together to form a heart on her chest. Inside the heart, someone had scrawled, *You will be missed.*

Altogether, the look made Levana want to gag.

"What do you want?" asked Levana, swinging her legs out from beneath the blankets.

"To see that you won't be embarrassing me by your appearance today." Reaching forward, Channary tugged at the flesh beneath Levana's eye, an experiment to see if the embedded gemstone would hold. Flinching, Levana knocked her hand away.

Channary smirked. "Thoughtful touch."

"Less fraudulent than claiming you're going to miss them," said Levana, glaring at the painted heart.

"Fraudulent? To the contrary. I shall miss them a great deal. Especially the parties that Father used to throw during the full Earth. And being able to borrow Mother's dresses when I was going shopping in AR-4." She hesitated. "Though I suppose now I can simply take her seamstress as my own, so perhaps that is no great loss after all." With a giggle, she sat down on the edge of the bed and snatched a berry from the breakfast tray, popping it onto her tongue. "You should be prepared to say a few words at the funeral today."

"*Me?*" It was an appalling idea. Everyone would be watching her, judging just how sad she was. She didn't think she could fake it well enough.

"You're their daughter too. And—" Suddenly, inexplicably choked up, Channary dabbed at the corner of her eye. "I don't think I'm strong enough to do it all on my own. I'll be overwhelmed by grief. Perhaps I will faint and require a guard to carry me to someplace dark and quiet to recover." She snorted, all signs of sadness vanishing as quickly as they had come. "That's an intriguing idea. Perhaps I can stage it to happen next to that new young one with the curly hair. He seems quite . . . obliging."

Levana scowled. "You're going to leave me alone to guide the entire kingdom in mourning, so that you can frolic with one of the guards?"

"Oh, stop it," said Channary, covering her ears. "You're so annoying when you whine."

"You're going to be *queen*, Channary. You're going to have to make speeches and important decisions that will affect everyone on Luna. Don't you think it's time you took that seriously?"

Laughing, Channary sucked at the grains of sugar left on her fingertips. "Like our parents took it so seriously?"

"Our parents are *dead*. Killed by a citizen who must not have thought they were doing a very good job."

Channary waved her hand through the air. "Being queen is a right, little sister. A right that comes with an endless supply of men and servants and beautiful dresses. Let the court and the thaumaturges deal with all the boring details. As for *me*, I am going to be known throughout history as the queen who never stopped laughing." Tossing her hair off her shoulder, she surveyed the bedroom, its gold-papered walls and hand-embroidered draperies. "Why aren't there any mirrors in here? I want to see how beautiful I look for my tear-filled performance."

Crawling from the bed, Levana pulled on a robe that had been laid out on the sitting chair. "You know very well why there aren't any mirrors."

To which Channary's grin widened. She hopped up from the bed as well. "Oh, yes, that's right. Your glamours are so becoming these days I'd almost forgotten."

Then, quick as a viper, Channary backhanded Levana across the face, sending her stumbling into one of the bedposts. Levana cried out, the shock causing her to lose control of her glamour.

"Ah, there's my ugly duckling," Channary cooed. Stepping closer, she grabbed Levana's chin, squeezing tight before Levana could raise her hand to soothe her already-flaming cheek. "I suggest you remember this the next time you think to contradict one of my orders. As you have so kindly reminded me, I am going to be queen, and I will not tolerate my commands being questioned, especially by my pathetic little sister. You *will* be speaking for me at the funeral."

Turning away, Levana blinked back the tears that had sprung up and scrambled to reinstate her illusion. To hide her disfigurements. To pretend that she was beautiful too.

Spotting movement in the corner of her eye, she saw a maid frozen in the doorway. Channary hadn't closed it upon entering, and Levana was quite certain the maid had seen everything.

Smartly, the servant lowered her gaze and curtsied.

Releasing Levana's chin, Channary stepped back. "Put on your mourning dress, little sister," she said, once again wearing her pretty smile. "We have a very big day ahead of us."

THE GREAT HALL WAS FILLED WITH GRAYS. GRAY HAIR, GRAY makeup, gray gloves, gray gowns, gray stockings. Charcoal jackets and heather sleeves, snowdrop shoes and stormy top hats. Despite the drab color palette, though, the funeral guests looked anything but mournful. For in those grays were gowns made of floating ribbons and sculpted jewelry and frosted flowers that grew like tiny gardens from bountiful poufed hair.

Levana could imagine that the Artemisian seamstresses had been kept very, *very* busy since the assassination.

Her own dress was adequate. A floor-length gown made of gray-on-gray damask velvet and a high lace neckline that, she guessed, looked lovely with the cropped black hair of her glamour. It was nothing as showy as Channary's tutu, but at least she maintained a bit of dignity.

On a dais at the front of the room, a holograph was showing the deceased king and queen as they had once looked in their summery youth. Her mother in her wedding gown—barely older then than Levana was now. Her father seated upon his throne, broad shouldered and square jawed. They were artist-rendered portraits, of course—recordings of the royal family were strictly prohibited—but the artist had captured their glamours almost perfectly. Her father's steely gaze, the graceful way her mother fluttered her fingers when she waved.

Levana stood beside Channary on the dais, accepting kisses on her hands and the condolences of Artemisia's families as they filtered past. Levana's stomach was in knots, knowing that Channary planned on shirking her duties as eldest and forcing her to give the speech. Though she had been practicing for years, Levana still had the irrational fear every time she addressed an audience that she would lose control of her glamour and they would see her as she truly was.

The rumors were bad enough. Whispers that the young princess was not at all beautiful, had in fact been grotesquely disfigured by some tragic accident in her childhood. That it was a mercy no one would ever have to look on her. That they were all lucky she was as skilled at her glamour as she was, so they wouldn't have to tolerate such ugliness in their precious court.

She bowed her head, thanking a woman for her lie about how very honorable her parents had been, when her attention caught on a man still a few persons back in the line.

Her heart tripped over itself. Her movements became automatic—nod, hold out your hand, mumble *thank you*—while all the world receded into a blur of grays.

Sir Evret Hayle had become a royal guard in her father's personal entourage when Levana was just eight years old, and she had loved him ever since, despite knowing that he was nearly ten years her senior. His skin was ebony dark, his eyes full of intelligence and cunning when he was on duty, and mirth when he was relaxed. She had once caught flecks of gray and emerald in his irises, and ever since was mesmerized by his eyes, hoping to be close enough one day to witness those flecks again. His hair was a mess of tightly coiled locks, long enough to seem unruly, short enough to be re-fined. Levana didn't think she'd ever seen him outside of his guard uniform, which very precisely indicated every muscle in his arms and shoulders—until today. He was wearing simple gray pants and a tunic-style shirt that was almost too relaxed for a royal funeral.

He wore them like a prince.

For seven years she had known him to be the most handsome man in the entire Lunar court. In the city of Arte-misia. On all of Luna. She had known it even before she was old enough to understand why her heart pounded so strongly when he was near.

And now he was coming closer. Only four people divid-ing them. Three. Two.

Hand beginning to tremble, Levana stood a little straighter and adjusted her glamour so that her eyes were a little brighter and the jewel in her skin glittered like an ac-tual tear. She made herself a bit taller too—closer to Evret's height, though still small enough to seem vulnerable and in need of protection.

It had been many months since she had reason to stand so near to him, and here he was, coming to her, with sympa-thy in his eyes. There were those flecks of gray and emerald, not a figment of her imagination after all. He was not playing the role of guard, for once, but of a mourning Lunar citizen.

He was taking her hand and raising it to his mouth, though the kiss landed in the air above her knuckles. Her pulse was an ocean in her ears.

"Your Highness," he said, and hearing his voice was almost as rare a treasure as seeing the flecks in his eyes. "I am so sorry for your loss. The sorrow belongs to us all, but I know you bear the weight more than anyone."

She tried to store his words away in the back of her mind, for retrieval and analysis at a moment when he was not holding her hand or peering into her soul. *I know you bear the weight more than anyone.*

Although he appeared honest, Levana didn't think he was overly fond of the king and queen. Perhaps his grief was because he'd not been on duty when the murders happened, so he couldn't have done anything to stop them. Levana sensed that he was exceptionally proud of his place on the royal guard.

For her part, though, she was grateful that Evret hadn't been there. That some other guards had been killed instead.

"Thank you," she breathed. "Your kindness makes this day easier to bear, Sir Hayle."

They were the same words she had said to countless other guests that day. Wishing she were clever enough to come up with something truly meaningful, she added, "I trust you know that you were a great favorite of my father's."

She had no idea whether it was true, but seeing Evret's eyes soften made it as true as she cared for it to be.

"I will continue to faithfully serve your family as long as I am able."

The proper words exchanged, he released her hand. Her skin tingled as she let it fall back to her side.

But rather than move on to offer condolences to Channary, Evret turned back and gestured to a woman beside him. "Your Highness, I do not believe you have ever met my wife. Her Royal Highness, Princess Levana Blackburn, this is Solstice Hayle. Sol, this is Her most charming Highness, Princess Levana."

Something shriveled up inside Levana, turning hard and sharp in her gut, but she forced herself to smile and offer her hand as Solstice curtsied and kissed her fingers and said something that Levana didn't hear. She knew that Evret had taken a wife some years ago, but she had given this fact little consideration. After all, her parents were married, but that had seemed to create no great affection between them, and what was a wife in a world in which mistresses were as common as servants, and monogamy as rare as an Earthen eclipse?

But now, meeting Evret's wife for the first time, she noticed three things in quick succession that made her reconsider every thought she'd had about this woman's existence.

First, that she was profoundly beautiful, but not in a glamoured sort of way. She had a cheerful, heart-shaped face, elegantly arched eyebrows, and honey-toned skin. She wore her hair loose for the occasion and it fell nearly to her waist in thick, dark strands that held just a bit of a curl.

Second, that Evret looked at her with a gentleness that Levana had never before seen in a man's eyes, and that look sparked a yearning in her so strong it felt like agony.

Third, that Evret's wife was very, very pregnant.

This, Levana had not known.

"It is lovely to meet you," Levana heard herself saying, though she didn't catch Solstice's response.

"Sol is a seamstress in AR-4," Evret said with pride in his voice. "She was commissioned to embroider some of the gowns worn today, even."

"Oh. Yes, I . . . I seem to recall my sister mentioning a seamstress in town who was becoming quite popular . . ." Levana trailed off as Solstice's entire face brightened, and the look only further solidified her own hatred.

Levana remembered nothing more from their brief conversation, until Evret placed his hand on his wife's back. The gesture seemed protective, and only as they continued on did Levana notice a fragility to Solstice that had at first been hidden by her beauty. She seemed a delicate creature, exhausted from the funeral or her pregnancy or both. Evret looked concerned as he whispered something to his wife, but Levana couldn't hear him, and Solstice was batting his attention away by the time they'd reached Channary.

Levana turned back to the receiving line. Another mourner, another well-wisher, another liar. Lies, all lies. Levana became a recording—nod, hold out your hand, mumble *thank you*—as the line stretched on and on. As her sister became less and less interested in pretending sadness and her giggles and flirtations tinkled shrilly above the low-voiced mutterings of the crowd, as the holograph of her parents accepted their wedding vows.

Monogamy. Faithfulness. *True love.* She did not think she had ever witnessed it, not beside the fairy tales she'd been told as a child and the fanciful dramas sometimes acted out for the court's entertainment. But to be so cherished—what a dream that must be. To have a man look upon you with such adoration. To feel the press of fingers on your back, a silent message to all who saw that you are his and he—he must be yours ...

When a woman with gray antlers on her head saw the tears beginning to glisten in Levana's eyes, she nodded understandingly and handed her a crisp gray handkerchief.

LEVANA CONVINCED HERSELF THAT IT WAS BOREDOM THAT drove her out of the palace three days after the funeral, still dressed in gray for the third and final day of mourning. She told herself that she wanted something bright and beautiful to wear when the mourning period was ended and all the kingdom rejoiced as their new queen took the throne for the first time. She told herself she needed a new pair of embroidered slippers for the coronation, or perhaps a finely spun scarf for her waist. Nothing in her wardrobe would suffice for such a historic occasion.

If she'd made up a story to tell to the guards at the maglev platforms, it was in vain. No one stopped her or asked where she was going.

AR-4, the most popular shopping district in Artemisia, was bustling with court families and nobles and their servants, all dressed in shades of gray, all making their arrangements for tomorrow's festivities, but no one recognized Levana, who was wearing the glamour of a dark-skinned goddess, tall and lithe, with a gracefully elongated neck and edged cheekbones. She did not bother with hair, not wanting to distract from the glamour's perfectly sculpted head and figure. Only the silent palace guards that followed in her wake would have given away her identity, but the street was too crowded for anyone to notice them or the girl they were tracking.

She paid no attention to the cobblers or the dress-makers, the milliners or the jewelers, the art galleries or the candy shoppes. She knew precisely where she was going. She counted the streets that she had seen on the holographic map that morning. Her eye caught briefly on the crescent Earth that could be seen in the black sky beyond the dome's protective sphere, but lost sight of it as she turned the corner into a lovely little side alley. The scent of roasting coffee from a small café followed her as she trotted around the flowering window boxes and stone-carved benches that lined the alley. Though it wasn't fully deserted, it was serene compared with the bustle of the main street.

There was the shop, just where the map and directory had indicated. A simple sign hung over the doorway, showing a needle and thread, and the paned window displayed an assortment of different yarns and fabrics.

As soon as she saw it, Levana realized that her stomach had knotted itself since turning into the alley. She was nervous.

And over what? The wife of a palace guard? A mere seamstress? Ridiculous.

She gestured for her guards to stay outside, braced herself, and pushed open the door.

She found herself in a well-lit showroom. A quick scan confirmed that no shopkeeper was present, but a second door was cracked open, leading to a back room where she could hear the whir of mechanical looms.

Two holographic mannequins in the corners were modeling a variety of garments—everything from lingerie to ball gowns, three-piece suits to crocheted stockings. Every piece was magnificent. It was easy to see how even this insignificant shop in a tiny alleyway in AR-4 was building such a quick reputation for itself among the families.

Levana paced around the showroom. It wasn't large, but there was a lot to see. Shelves stacked with embroidered towels, bed linens, and window draperies. Silk scarves so delicate they felt like spiderwebs. A dress form wore a corset-style bodice that appeared to have been woven entirely of fine silver thread and tiny sparkling gems—it was jewelry as much as it was clothing.

Then she spotted a quilt that hung on one wall, large enough to take up almost the entire space. Levana stepped back to admire it, enchanted.

Earth. And space. Pieced together from shredded fabrics of all different sizes and shapes, the edges left raw where they'd been seamed together. Shining forest greens and rough-textured desert browns, shimmering ocean blues and velvet ebony blacks, all stitched together with gold thread. Every segment of the quilt was embroidered with whimsical patterns of ivy and flowers, elaborate spiral curls and glowing starbursts, and though it seemed like it should have been chaotic and excessive, the consistency of the gold thread grounded the piece. Made it beautiful and somehow serene. Levana knew very little about quilting or embroidery, but she could tell, instinctually, that every tiny stitch had been done by hand.

"Hello."

Levana gasped and checked—first—that her glamour hadn't faded with her distraction, before turning around.

Solstice Hayle stood at the door to the back room, a smile on her lips and an embroidery hoop holding a swath of white cotton in her hand. A needle had been secured in the corner of the material, dark maroon thread strung through its eye.

"Can I help you?"

She looked like the embodiment of kindness, in a way that made Levana instantly defensive.

"Yes. I—" She hesitated, forgetting why she was there. What had possessed her to come to this shop, to see this beautiful woman and her enormous stomach and all the lovely garments she made with her own skilled fingers?

She swallowed down the rising despair. Remembered that *she* was beautiful too, so long as her glamour held. Remembered that *she* was a princess. "I need something for tomorrow," she said. "To wear to the coronation."

Solstice nodded. "Of course. I'm afraid anything constructed brand-new for the occasion would have to be
rushed, which I try to avoid. But perhaps we can find something you like here in the showroom and alter it to fit your
tastes." She set aside the embroidery hoop, her hand moving
to rest on her stomach as she waddled around the room.
"Were you wanting a gown? Or perhaps some accessories?"

After a moment's thought, Levana answered, "Do you
have any gloves?" She already had plenty, but gloves wouldn't
have to be sized. And she liked wearing gloves. They made
for one less thing she had to hide with her glamour.

"Oh, yes, I have a wonderful assortment of gloves."

Balancing with one hand on the edge of a wooden
dresser, Solstice bent over to pull out one of the lower draw-
ers. It was filled with women's gloves, each neatly folded atop
a layer of tissue paper. "Will you be wearing a glamour for the
occasion?"

Levana stiffened. "What do you mean?"

Solstice glanced up in surprise, and Levana sucked in
a breath, realizing that her palms were sweating. She was
suddenly *angry*. Angry that this woman was so effortlessly
pretty. Angry that tonight she would sleep beside her doting
husband. That soon she would hold a wrinkled, wailing baby
in her arms and that child would never question whether it
was loved, or whether its parents loved each other.

Nothing Levana wanted had ever come that easily.

Solstice must have noticed a darkness lurking in Levana's eyes. She stood up, her expression showing the first hints of caution. She was breathing heavier than before, as if the small motion of opening the drawer had exhausted her, and there was a bead of sweat on her upper lip. She certainly was a fragile thing, wasn't she?

And yet her gentle smile never left. "I only meant that if you'll be using a glamour, we can pick out a color that will complement your chosen skin tone. Or ... if you already know what gown you'll be wearing, we can coordinate the two."

Trying to smother the envy that had stoked inside her chest, Levana looked down at her hands. The long, slender fingers and flawless skin that weren't really hers.

Wetting her lips, she met Solstice's gaze again. "What would you choose for yourself?"

Solstice quirked her head to one side, reminding Levana of the small birds in the palace menagerie when they heard an unfamiliar sound and mistook it for a predator.

Solstice returned her attention to the drawer of gloves. "Well ...," she said uncertainly. "I've always been fond of jewel tones, myself." Crouching again, she peeled back a couple layers of tissue paper and emerged with a set of silk gloves in rich sapphire blue. Though the gloves themselves were undecorated, their tops were rimmed with small gold chains and each had a tiny metal clasp. Levana guessed that they would reach almost to her shoulders. Solstice held the gloves against Levana's wrist, showing the contrast with her dark skin. "What do you think?"

Pressing her lips together, Levana ran her thumb over the gold clasps. "What are these for?"

"It's part of a new design I've been working on. It's meant to be a set. See, they go with this necklace . . ." She led Levana to a jewelry counter lined with chains and beads and fasteners, and gestured at a gold collar. At first Levana assumed it was made of metal, but when she picked it up, she realized that it was tightly woven gold thread, intricately braided together and flexible in her grip. Two more clasps were attached to it on opposite sides. Sol continued, "I have small filigree chains that connect it to the gloves, see?"

Levana did see. It was beautiful and unusual, two things that were always popular in court fashion, but not gaudy as Levana found so many of the trendy pieces to be.

She trailed her fingers over the braided threads and imagined wearing it on her neck. How regal she would look. How it would accentuate her throat and collarbone, how the deep blue silk would look so stunning against her honey skin and rich brown hair.

Only then did she realize that in the fantasy, she looked like Solstice Hayle.

She set down the necklace, and Solstice gestured back to the dresser. "Would you like to see the other gloves?"

"No," said Levana. "I'll take these. And the necklace too."

"Oh—wonderful! Will you . . . do you want to take them with you today, or did you want them to be personalized?"

"Personalized?"

Solstice nodded. "That's what I specialize in—the little flourishes that, I like to think, set my shop apart from all the other seamstresses in Artemisia. If there's a particular design you'd like embroidered on the gloves, I should be able to have them done by tomorrow morning. Some of my clients like to get their favorite flower, or their initials . . ."

Levana glanced at the quilt of Earth that hung on the wall. "You did that, didn't you?"

"Yes, I did." Solstice laughed, and her laughter was surprisingly giddy, like a child's. "Although it took much longer than a single evening. Do you like it?"

Levana frowned. She did like it, very much. But she didn't want to say so.

"You can embroider the gloves for me," she said. "I want the design to be something whimsical, like you did in the quilt. Maybe something with an *L* in it, but nothing too obvious."

"An *L*? Like Luna." Her smile was back, as warm as ever. "I'd be happy to. Shall I have it delivered in the morning?"

"Yes." Levana paused, before squaring her shoulders. "Have it delivered to the palace. Address it to Princess Levana, and I will let the stewards know that I am expecting a delivery. They will see that you receive payment."

Solstice's smile froze, her eyes caught between surprise and panic. Levana knew the look well, the look when any of the palace servants realized they'd been in the presence of royalty and their minds skittered to recall if they'd said or done anything worth punishing. Gathering herself, Solstice gave a half curtsy, using the countertop to keep her balance. "I am sorry I didn't recognize you, Your Highness. It is such an incredible honor to be in your service."

Heated by the knowledge of her power over this insignificant woman and her insignificant shop, bolstered by the thought that it was, indeed, an *honor* to serve her, Levana was tempted to demonstrate her authority. She imagined demanding that Solstice kneel to her, knowing it couldn't be easy in her condition. Or threatening her business's reputation should she be displeased with the gloves when they arrived. Or suggesting that Solstice *give* her the marvelous quilt of Earth, as a royal tithe, or a symbol of gratitude, and watching her struggle to give up something that clearly had so much value—to her, and to her livelihood.

But Levana buried the fantasies before her tongue could betray her.

Solstice would surely tell her husband, and then Evret Hayle would never again refer to Levana as *Her most charming Highness.*

She gulped, hard, and forced a smile for the first time since stepping into the shop. Perhaps this was why she'd come. So that Solstice would tell her husband about the princess's unexpected visit, and that Levana would even be wearing one of her designs to the coronation. Levana's heart warmed to think that Evret would know what a generous princess she was. She wanted him to think about her, even if only for a moment. She wanted him to admire her.

And so, she lied. "The honor will be all mine," she said, "in wearing such an exquisite piece. I can see why Sir Hayle has sung your praises so highly."

Solstice flushed with all the joy of a woman in love, and Levana left, quickly, before her own bile could burn her throat.

BY THE NEXT MORNING, ON THE DAY OF CHANNARY'S coronation, it seemed that all of Luna had been granted permission to pretend that the assassinations had never happened, that the memories of King Marrok and Queen Jannali would live on peaceably in their history texts, and that young Channary would make for a most fair and just ruler. Levana wasn't sure how many people believed this, and no doubt those who did had never met her sister, but Channary's right to the throne went unquestioned even by her. They were, after all, the only known heirs of the Blackburn bloodline, that distant ancestor who had been first born with the Lunar gift. Channary, as the eldest royal daughter, would be queen, as her son or daughter would rule next, and the generation after that, and the generation after that. It was how the crown had been passed on since the day Luna became a monarchy, since the day Cyprus Blackburn created his own throne.

Levana would not be the one to disrupt those values now, no matter how much it irked her to know that silly, vapid Channary would spend more time batting her lashes at handsome servants than discussing the economic difficulties facing their country.

But Levana was only fifteen years old, as she was so often reminded, so what did she know about it?

Nothing at all, is what Channary would say, or any one of the thaumaturges who were preparing to swear fealty to her. Their bias seemed to ignore the laws, that Lunar royalty could rule as young as thirteen, with or without the advice of a council.

Levana stood on the third-level balcony, staring down into the great hall where the funeral had been, where her sister had sobbed until she could hardly breathe and then fainted, or pretended to faint, and was carried away by—of all the guards—Evret Hayle, who was standing nearby when it happened. Where Levana had been left alone to blunder through an unprepared speech of lies and fake tears.

The grays were gone now, replaced with the official colors of Luna—white, red, and black. An enormous tapestry hung on the wall behind the dais, depicting the Lunar insignia in shimmering, handwoven threads, a design that had originated back when Luna was a republic. It depicted Luna and the capital city of Artemisia in the foreground, with Earth—once their ally—in the distance. It was a majestic piece, but it was impossible for Levana not to think that it would have been even more stunning had it been made by the fingers of Solstice Hayle.

Though countless servants were toiling away in preparation for the ceremony, and her sister was no doubt being fitted into her gown at that moment, Levana was glad for the temporary serenity in the empty hall.

She had selected a simple sapphire-blue dress to match the gloves delivered to her chambers that morning. They arrived in a white box, wrapped in crisp tissue paper and accompanied by a little note from Solstice, which Levana had thrown away without reading.

The gloves were even more beautiful in the daylight that poured through the palace windows, and the embroidery was more delicate and exquisite than she'd imagined. The threads began with flourishing Ls placed covertly on her palms, before curling around her forearms and past her elbows like living vines that then blended perfectly with the chains that continued on to her neck.

She almost felt like a queen standing there, and she couldn't keep away a fantasy that she was the one being crowned that day. She hadn't yet decided on an acceptable glamour for the occasion, so in that moment, she became her sister. Twenty-two years old, mature and elegant, with those ever-smiling eyes.

But no. She didn't want to be Channary. She didn't want her beauty, not if it came with her cruelty and selfishness as well.

No sooner had she thought it than another woman flashed through her thoughts.

I do not believe you have ever met my wife.

Trying on the glamour of Solstice Hayle felt like something taboo and reprehensible, and strangely *right* in the very wrongness of it. Levana thought of her flawless complexion and the ringlets of dark hair draped over her shoulders, of her almond-shaped eyes and the way her lips had a just-kissed hint of rouge to them, though the idea that the redness was caused by a kiss was quite possibly a product of Levana's own envy. She thought of Solstice's thick, flirtatious eyelashes, and how she had seemed to glow with happiness, even on a day of mourning. She thought of Solstice's stomach, plump and round with the promise of a child.

Evret's child.

Levana settled a hand on her own stomach, incorporating the pregnancy into the glamour. What must that feel like, to have a living creature growing inside her? A child created by love, not political advantage or manipulation.

"Levana, are you up—"

Gasping, Levana spun around as Channary crested the top of the staircase. Her sister saw her and paused. "Oh, you're not ..."

Channary hesitated, her eyes narrowing. It was an expression that Levana had seen a thousand times. No matter how confident she was becoming in her glamours, Channary always saw through them. She would never explain what Levana was giving away, whether it was the way she held herself or a particular expression or some other tell, like a gambler's tick. But Channary had a special knack for discovering it.

Sensing that Channary hadn't yet made up her mind about the pregnant woman loitering on the great hall's upper balcony, Levana dipped into a humble curtsy.

"I do beg your pardon, Your Highness," she said in her meekest voice. "I should not be up here. I was only waiting for my husband to get off duty and thought I would come to admire the decorations."

Thinking she had already said more than a real seamstress would, Levana curtsied again. "May I take my leave of you, Your Highness?"

"Yes," said Channary, still hesitant, "and don't let me catch you up here again. This isn't a playground for the desperately bored. If you need something useful to occupy your time while you're"—she gestured at Levana's stomach—"reproducing, I'm sure my lady's maid can find something for you to do. There will be no idleness under my rule, not even for women of your condition."

"Of course, Your Highness." Keeping her head bowed, Levana ducked around her sister and darted toward the steps.

"One more thing."

She froze, a mere three steps lower than where Channary stood, and dared not meet her gaze.

"You are Sir Hayle's wife, aren't you?"

"Yes, Your Highness."

She heard a soft footstep, and another, as Channary came to stand on the step above her. Curious, Levana dared to glance upward, regretting it the moment she saw Channary's smirk.

"Do tell him how much I enjoyed our time together after the funeral," said Channary, her voice lilting over the words like a stream bubbling over worn stones. "He was such a *comfort* to me, and I hope we can enjoy each other's company again soon." Her tongue darted through the corner of her mouth as she admired the fake pregnancy bump. "You are a *very* lucky woman, Mrs. Hayle."

Levana's jaw fell, horror and indignation filling her head as quickly as hot blood rushed to her face. "You're lying!"

Channary's insinuating look turned immediately to arrogance. "It *is* you!" she said, laughing delightedly. "What in the name of Luna are you doing impersonating a guard's wife? And a pregnant one at that!"

Balling her hands into fists, Levana turned and marched down the steps. "I'm only practicing!" she called over her shoulder.

"Practicing your glamour?" Channary said, traipsing after her. "Or practicing for a life of eternal loneliness? You must know you're not going to catch the eye of anyone in court by prancing around as a poor, pregnant woman. Or—oh!" Faking a gasp, Channary clapped a hand over her mouth.

"Are you hoping that Sir Hayle himself sees you like this? Do you have fantasies of him mistaking you for his beloved? Swooping you into his arms, kissing you breathless, perhaps even . . . *reenacting* what led to your present condition?"

Smothering her embarrassment, Levana kept a firm hold on the glamour of Solstice Hayle, in part for the principle of it. Channary thought that if she taunted Levana enough, she could control her decisions, and Levana refused to let that be true.

"Stop it," she seethed, arriving at the first landing. She rounded a carved column to continue down to the ground floor, her hand rested on her stomach like a real pregnant woman might do. "You're only jealous because you never have any originality with your—"

She froze halfway down the steps.

Two guards stood at attention on the lower landing.

One of them was Evret Hayle.

A shudder pulsed through her, from her very empty womb up through her chest and vibrating down through her gloved fingertips.

Despite all his training, Evret was failing at keeping his expression stoic and disinterested. He gaped at Levana— Solstice—and he tried so very, very hard to look professional, but it was conflicted and confused.

"Solstice?" he stammered, brow furrowed as he took in

the beautiful blue dress that pulled tight over her stomach, the elaborately embroidered gloves that he'd no doubt seen his wife working on the evening before. "You're supposed to be resting. What are you doing here?"

Levana gulped and wished and wished and wished that she were truly his beloved.

"Oops," said Channary. "I guess I should have told you he was down here. Completely slipped my mind." She drifted down the steps until she was standing beside Levana and placed a hand on Levana's shoulder. "Don't worry, you silly man. This is my baby sister, only pretending to be your wife." She dropped her voice into an exuberant whisper. "Between you and me, I think she might have a bit of a crush on you. Isn't that just darling?"

Levana felt a sob in the base of her throat, clawing to get out, and knew it would succeed if she stood there a moment longer. She tried to figure out what was the worst part of this moment. That Evret had seen her impersonating his wife, or that he might have heard Channary's accusations.

She decided it was all mortifying. She decided she would rather have been stabbed sixteen times in the chest than have to live through this one excruciating moment.

Shoving Channary away, she hid her face—her beautiful, flawless, beloved face—and ran from the hall. Ran as fast as she could, ignoring the protective guards that hastened to keep up with her, ignoring the servants that threw themselves against walls to be out of her way.

She started ripping off the gloves the second she reached her private chambers. One of the chains snapped. The hem on the other glove ripped. She unclasped the gold-braided necklace, nearly choking herself in her need to get it off.

The dress was next, and she didn't care if she shredded it. She *wanted* to ruin it. Soon, the gown and the gloves were wadded into a tight ball and thrust into the corner of her wardrobe, and she knew she would never put them on again.

She was so stupid. Such a stupid, stupid girl.

For ever thinking she could be admired. For ever thinking she could be beautiful, or adored, or noticed. For ever thinking she could be anything at all.

LEVANA ATTENDED THE CORONATION CEREMONY IN HEAD-to-toe white, under the guise of a waxen-haired princess with skin so pale as to be almost invisible, her faded glamour hiding the tracks of her tears.

She sat in the front row and praised her sister when the rest of the gathered Lunars praised her, and knelt when the rest of Luna knelt, and bowed her head with all the others. She refused to look at Channary, not even when the crown was placed on her head or when she took the scepter in her hand or the great white cloak was draped over her shoulders. Not when she drank the blood of her people from a golden chalice or when she cut open her fingertip and let her own blood splatter into an ornate marble bowl or when she spoke the vows that Levana knew Channary would never take to heart.

She also did not look at Evret, though he was on duty and stood directly within her line of sight throughout the proceedings.

Levana was a statue. A girl carved of regolith and dust.

She hated her sister, now her queen. Her sister did not deserve the throne. She would squander every opportunity she had to make a great ruler. To increase the economic potential of Luna. To continue the research and technological advancements that their ancestors had begun. To make Artemisia the most beautiful and enviable city in the galaxy.

Her sister did not deserve that scepter. That cloak. That crown.

She deserved nothing.

But she would have it all. She and Solstice Hayle and all the families of the court would have everything they ever wanted.

Only Levana—too young and ugly to matter—would go

on living in her sister's shadow until she faded away and everyone forgot that she'd ever been there to begin with.

SHE TURNED SIXTEEN TWO WEEKS LATER. THE COUNTRY celebrated, but on the heels of the week-long party that had come from the coronation, the birthday seemed to dissolve into just one more day of royal shenanigans. An illusionist was hired to perform at the feast, and he awed the court's families with feats of magic and wonderment, and the partygoers were more than willing to be taken with his pretend fancies.

Levana attended her own birthday celebration as the pale, invisible girl. She sat at the head table beside her beautiful sister and pretended not to notice how the illusionist turned a tablecloth into a lion and a lady's handkerchief into a rabbit, and the crowd oohed and aahed and placed jovial bets as the lion chased the rabbit under tables and around their ankles. Then the pretend rabbit hopped up into the queen's lap, who giggled and went to stroke the long floppy ears, and the creature vanished. The napkin, still held in the illusionist's hand, was nothing but a napkin.

The lion bowed to the queen, before he, too, disappeared. A tablecloth untouched.

The crowd was in fits, applauding and laughing.

No one seemed to care that every illusion had been centered before the queen, not the birthday girl.

After a series of flourishing bows, the illusionist took a tapered candle from one of the tables and blew it out. The crowd fell silent. Levana sensed that she was the only person who didn't lean forward in curiosity.

He let the black smoke curl naturally for a moment, before arranging it into a pair of entangled lovers. Two naked bodies, writhing against each other.

The show of debauchery received boisterous laughter from the families, and flirtatious smiles from the queen.

It was easy to tell who would be warming her sister's bed that night.

For her part, Levana could feel the heat burning in her cheeks, though she hid her mortification behind the pale-faced glamour. Not that such entertainment was anything shocking, but while the illusion persisted, she could feel Evret's presence in the room like a gravitational pull. The knowledge that he was seeing the same suggestive show, listening to the same bawdy laughter, possibly thinking of his own relations with his wife, made Levana feel as pathetic and insignificant as a crumb off her own cake.

She had not spoken to Evret since he witnessed her impersonating Solstice, which was not altogether unusual—they had shared more words at the funeral than in the entire time she'd known him. But she couldn't shake away the suspicion that he was avoiding her, perhaps as much as she was avoiding him.

Levana assumed he must still be mortified, both at her glamour and at Channary's accusations. But she couldn't avoid a fantasy that maybe he was also flattered. Maybe he had begun to notice how his heart fluttered extra fast when he saw her. Maybe he was regretting marriage, or realizing that marriage was as silly a convention as many of the court families believed it to be, and that he loved her . . . he had always loved her, but now he didn't know what to do with those emotions.

It was a very complex fantasy, which frequently left her even more depressed than she'd been before.

The smoke charade faded away to loud cheers, and the illusionist had not finished his bow before every candle flame on the head table exploded.

Levana screamed, tipping backward so fast that her chair crashed to the floor, bringing her with it. Though the flames continued to roar above her, bright and flickering, she realized after a terrified moment that there was no heat coming from them. Neither the threatening pulse of fire nor the smell of charred flesh followed.

No one else had screamed.

No one else had tried to get away.

Now, everyone was laughing.

Trembling, Levana accepted the hand of one of the royal guards—they alone were not showing their amusement. Her chair was righted, and she settled self-consciously back onto it.

The flames continued to burn, every one of them now as tall as a person, and with her terror waning, Levana was able to discern that this was just another illusion. Hovering over the table of wine goblets and half-finished plates was a line of fiery dancers, twirling and leaping from candlestick to candlestick.

Channary was laughing harder than all the others. "Whatever is the matter, baby sister?" *Come here, baby sister.* "You can't possibly be afraid of a silly little trick." *I want to show you something.*

Levana found that she couldn't respond. Her heart was still thumping wildly, and her distrustful gaze was still fixed on the flame-dancers. Their existence, even if only a mental trick created by manipulating her own bioelectricity, made it impossible for her to relax. She could not tear her attention from them. Which was fine. She didn't wish to see the mocking expressions around her. Hearing the laughter was bad enough.

She was only grateful that she'd had enough practice with the glamour of the invisible girl that she hadn't lost her control.

"Is the princess afraid of fire?" asked the illusionist. Though he didn't stop the illusion, the dancers did stop jumping, instead content to twirl slowly upon each candle-wick. "I apologize, Your Highness. I did not know."

"Don't worry about her," said Channary, holding a hand toward one of the dancers. "We cannot let her childish fears ruin our fun."

"Ah—do be careful, Your Majesty. The fire underneath is still very real." To prove his point, the illusionist sent the nearest dancer stepping down off her candle and into Channary's palm, leaving the very real flame still flickering behind. Again, the crowd *oohed* its pleasure, and again Levana was forgotten.

Don't worry about her.

It was only her birthday, after all. This was only her party.

The performance ended with all of the dancers turning into old-fashioned rocket ships that blasted upward and exploded into fireworks.

Once the delighted crowd had finished applauding, the dessert course was served. Levana stared down at the chocolate torte with the sugar sculpture that rose up nearly an arm's length above her plate, a delicate series of curls and filigree. It looked as though it would shatter with a single touch.

Levana did not pick up her fork.

She wasn't hungry. Her stomach was still in knots over the explosion of fire. She could feel her palms sweating beneath the glamour, and that was the sort of detail that was hard to ignore and could weaken a person's focus. Having already embarrassed herself, she would *not* let these people see beneath her glamour too.

"I'm going to bed," she said, to no one in particular. If anyone had been paying attention to her, if anyone had cared, they would have heard. But no one did.

She glanced at Channary, who had called the illusionist over to their table and was feeding him a forkful of chocolate.

Levana wondered what the illusionist looked like beneath his glamour. He was handsome now, but beneath the surface, he could be anyone.

They could all be anyone.

Why couldn't she be *anyone*? Why couldn't she be the one person she wanted to be?

Perhaps the trouble was that she could never quite figure out who that person was.

She pushed her chair out, reveling in the loud screech of legs on the hard floor.

No one looked her way.

It was not until she had left the dining hall and was alone in the main corridor that someone stopped her.

"Your Highness?"

She turned back to see that a guard had followed her into the corridor. Well—three guards, but only two of them were assigned to follow her at a respectful distance and ensure she wasn't threatened en route to her chambers.

This third guard was familiar, but only in the way that she knew he had served beneath her parents for some years.

"What is it?"

He bowed. "Forgive my intrusion, Highness. My friend, Sir Evret Hayle, asked me to give you this. With joyful birthday wishes."

He produced a small box, wrapped in plain brown paper.

Her heart twisted and she found that she couldn't approach him to take the gift.

"Evret Hayle?"

He nodded.

It's a trick, it's a trick, it's a trick. Her mind repeated the warning over and over. This was something her sister had set up. Some cruel diversion.

But her heart fluttered anyway. Her pulse boiled and rushed.

She dared a glance through the enormous doors back into the dining hall. Evret was stationed at the far end of the hall, but he was smiling kindly at her. As she stared, he placed a fist to his heart, a respectful salute that could have meant nothing.

Or could have meant everything.

It was all the confirmation she needed.

"Thank you," she said, snatching the box away.

The guard bowed and returned to his post.

It took all of Levana's willpower not to run to her chambers. A maid was there already, waiting to help her undress and wash for bed, but Levana shooed her out without even bothering to have her dress unpinned. Sitting at her mirror-less vanity, she forced herself to pause and to breathe, so that she could remove the plain paper with utmost delicacy. Her fingers trembled as she undid the fastenings, uncrinkled the corners.

Inside the box were shreds of more brown paper and, nestled among them, a small pendant of planet Earth. Silver, perhaps, though it was tarnished and bent. It seemed very old.

There was also a card, hand-printed with dreadful penmanship.

Your Royal Highness,
I hope that giving you a birthday gift will
not be seen as overstepping my station,
but I saw this and thought you might like
it. May you have only happiness in this
your seventeenth year.
   Your friend, and most loyal servant,
Evret Hayle

A note was added to the bottom, almost as an after-thought,

My wife also sends her warmest regards.

Before she knew what she was doing, Levana had torn off the bottom part of the card, ripping away the mention of his wife and shredding it into tiny pieces. Then she lifted the pendant from the box and cradled it against her chest, smiling, while she read Evret's words again and again. Interpreting. Dissecting. Again and again and again.

"I'M PLEASED TO REPORT THAT OUR BIOENGINEERING research and development team has been making great progress these past months," said Head Thaumaturge Joshua Haddon, standing before the queen's throne and the audience of aristocrats with his hands tucked into his wide sleeves. "Dr. Darnel believes that the latest advancements in bioelectrical pulse manipulation will result in the successful alteration of natural instincts. With Your Majesty's approval, the team intends to commence testing on Lunar subjects within the next twelve months."

Channary popped a fried squash blossom into her mouth and waved her hand at the thaumaturge. After swallowing, she licked the butter from her fingertips. "Yes, fine. Whatever they think."

"Then it shall be done, My Queen." Checking his report, Thaumaturge Haddon proceeded to the next matter of business, something to do with a method for increasing productivity in the textile sectors.

Levana wanted to know more about the soldiers. She had heard talk of the ongoing development of bioengineered soldiers for years now. It was a program her father started, perhaps a decade ago, and many of the families snubbed it as a ridiculous concept. Create an army that relied not on their Lunar gift, but on animal instincts? Ludicrous, they called it. Absurd. Monstrous.

Her father had rather liked that description, Levana

recalled. *Monstrous* was precisely what he meant to achieve, and the research commenced by order of the king. Though he was not alive to see his efforts come to fruition, Levana was intrigued by his fantasy.

An entire army of half-men, half-beast creatures. Soldiers who had the intelligence of humans, but the sensory perception of wild predators. They wouldn't fight by expected and predictable means of warfare, but rather by the basest instincts of hunting and survival to terrorize and pillage and devour their enemies.

The thought gave Levana a chill all along her spine, and not in a bad way. The temptation to control the sort of animalistic strength these soldiers would have made her mouth water. With that sort of power she could forever quiet the mockery that followed her in the palace corridors, the ongoing rumors about the pathetic, ugly little princess.

"Fine, fine," said Channary through a yawn, interrupting the thaumaturge mid-sentence. "Whatever you think is best. Are we almost finished?"

Joshua Haddon didn't seem at all put off by the queen's lack of interest in public policy and her country's welfare, though it took all of Levana's efforts to keep from rolling her eyes. Despite the occasional distracted thoughts, she legitimately wanted to know what was going on in the outer sectors. *She* wanted to hear the court's ideas for improvement. Perhaps they could simply send Channary off for her afternoon nap and allow Levana to handle the rest.

Though everyone would have laughed her to shreds if she'd suggested such a thing.

"Only one more issue to discuss, My Queen, before we adjourn."

Channary sighed.

"As I'm sure you are aware, My Queen, our previous rulers, may they rest ever in divine luxury, were in the process of developing a biochemical weapon that we have reason to believe could be quite effective in any negotiation efforts with Earth, especially given our ongoing antagonistic relationship and the possibility that it could someday dissolve into violence."

"Oh, stars *above*," said Channary, throwing her head back with an overwrought groan. "Is all this jargon necessary? Out with it, Joshua. What is your point?"

The members of the court sniggered behind their dainty hands.

Thaumaturge Haddon stood a little straighter. "One of our laboratories has concocted a contagious disease that we believe—though are yet unable to test—would be fatal to Earthens. As our relationship with Earth has been growing increasingly hostile and may continue to worsen if we're not able to enter into an alliance and reinstate open trade agreements within the next decade, King Marrok thought this disease could be a means of weakening any Earthen opposition, both in numbers and resources."

"And I'm sure my father was entirely correct. You may proceed with your ... research. *Adjourned.*"

"I must ask for one more moment of your valuable time, My Queen."

Huffing, Channary sank back into her seat. "What?"

"There is still the issue of an antidote."

When he didn't offer further explanation, Channary shrugged at him.

"As tempting as it may be to one day release this disease on Earth with no concerns for repercussions," explained Haddon, "some strategists, myself included, feel that an even stronger statement would be to let Earth believe the disease is an act of fate, even punishment. And that should we then offer them an antidote as a means to rid themselves of the disease, it could be the factor that ensures any future alliance discussions being swayed in our direction."

"You want to make them sick," Channary said, slowly and tiredly, "and then you want to make them better? That is the stupidest war tactic I've ever heard."

"No, it isn't," said Levana. The attention of a hundred members of the royal court turned to her, along with the sudden burning gaze of her sister, peering down from her throne. Levana squared her shoulders and refused to be intimidated. "They wouldn't need to know that the disease had come from us. It would be the best type of warfare—the type that no one *thinks* is warfare at all. We could weaken Earth without risking any retaliation." Tearing her focus from the thaumaturge, she looked up at Channary to find that her sister was spilling venom from her eyes. It didn't bother Levana, though. She had seen the potential where Channary had not. "And then, once they are so downtrodden as to pose no threat to us in the event of full-on war, we open peaceful negotiations. We make our demands, and we offer the one thing they want more than anything else—an antidote to the disease that has crippled them. It would be seen as the ultimate show of goodwill, not only that we have been using our own resources to develop the antidote, but that we would offer to manufacture and distribute it to them, our previous enemies. How could they say no to any of our requests?"

"That is precisely the strategy we suggest," said Thaumaturge Haddon. "The young princess stated it very clearly, thank you."

Despite the kindness of his words, something in his tone made Levana feel chastised. Like her presence in these meetings was barely tolerated as it was, and certainly no one had invited her to *contribute* to them.

"I suppose I see the potential," said Channary, toying with a lock of hair. "You may continue with developing this antidote."

"That is precisely the conundrum we've crossed, My Queen."

She raised an eyebrow. "Of course there's a conundrum, isn't there?"

"We have already found a means of developing an antidote, and its effectiveness against the infected microbes has been successfully proven through multiple tests. However, that antidote is developed using the blood cells of ungifted Lunars."

"Shells?"

"Yes, My Queen. Shells contain the necessary antibodies for the antidote production. Unfortunately, it has proven both timely and costly to obtain blood samples from shells when their population is so widely scattered throughout the outer sectors, and artificial duplication has thus far not been successful."

"Well then, why don't you cage them up like the animals they are? We'll call it retribution for the assassinations of my parents." A new glint entered Channary's eyes. "That's quite brilliant, actually. Let everyone know how dangerous shells are, and that the crown will no longer tolerate the leniency we've given them over the years. We can enact a new law if that will help."

Thaumaturge Haddon nodded. "I think this is a wise course of action, My Queen. To date, Thaumaturge Sybil Mira has been the court's ambassador with the biochemical research team. Perhaps she is a good candidate to begin drawing up a procedure for the best means of obtaining the blood samples."

A young woman stepped out of the line of thaumaturges, dressed in a maroon-red coat, with glossy raven's-wing hair falling down her back. She was beautiful in the way that all members of the queen's entourage were beautiful, but there was also something admirable in the way she held herself. A confidence that glimmered. Though her station was beneath the head thaumaturge, her posture and faint smile seemed to indicate that she didn't much believe herself to be beneath anyone at all.

Levana liked her immediately.

"Agreed. I deem Thaumaturge . . . er . . ."

"Sybil Mira, My Queen," she said.

"Mira as the official royal representative of . . . oh, I don't know." Channary sighed. "Ungifted affairs. You have my permission, by royal decree, to do what needs to be done for the betterment of . . . everyone." Channary's fingers danced whimsically through the air as she strung the words together, more like she was composing a pretty-sounding poem than issuing a decree that could impact the lives of hundreds of citizens—thousands, once their families were taken into account.

Still, the thaumaturges bowed respectfully when she finished and, finally, court was adjourned. The audience stood with the queen, but before leaving, Channary fixed her sweet smile on Levana.

"Dear baby sister," she cooed. *Come here, baby sister.* Levana flinched before she could brace herself, but if Channary noticed, she didn't show it. "I have a fitting with my seamstress this afternoon. Why don't you come with me? It would benefit you to have some gowns that aren't quite so . . . sad."

Levana didn't need to look down at her pale yellow dress, or to see how the color faded into her pale glamoured skin, to know what Channary was talking about. She had lost interest in being noticed. Let Channary be known for how fair and mirthful she was. Princess Levana would earn respect in the court by being intelligent and resourceful. By meeting the needs of her country when the queen was too busy cavorting with her many suitors to care.

"I am not in need of a new gown, thank you, My Queen."

"Fine, don't try anything on, then. You will make an excellent hat stand while I'm being fitted. Come along."

She smothered a groan, the thought of denying her sister already exhausting her.

Channary swooped ahead, and the thaumaturges and aristocrats all bowed. Walking in her sister's wake, Levana imagined that she was the one they were really bowing to.

As she followed her sister into the palace corridor, she spotted Evret coming toward them. Her heart pattered, but Evret didn't even look at her, merely stopped and saluted the queen as she passed, one fist clapped over his chest. Levana tried to catch his eye, but he stared at the wall over her head, expressionless as a statue.

Only when she glanced back a few steps later did she realize he had come to change shifts with one of the other guards. The changing of the guard was fast and smooth, like a well-oiled clock. Gulping, Levana faced forward again, lest she walk into a wall. This could be her chance to thank him for the pendant that was, even then, hanging around her neck, tucked beneath the collar of her dress.

She could hear Evret's boots clacking behind her. Feel his presence tugging her toward him. The back of her neck tingled, and she imagined him looking at her. Admiring the curvature of her neck. His gaze dropping intimately down her back.

Her emotions were in tatters by the time they had reached the main corridor of the palace and turned to begin the climb toward Her Majesty's quarters on the top floor. Channary did not like to take the elevators. She had once told Levana that she felt queenly having to lift her skirts as she went up and down the stairs.

It had taken all of Levana's efforts not to ask if that was the same reason she lifted her skirts all those other times too.

"Your Majesty?"

Channary paused, and Levana came to a stumbling halt behind her. Turning, she saw a girl not much older than she was, dressed in plain utilitarian clothes. She was breathless and flushed, her hair falling out of a loose bun in messy chunks.

"I do apologize for my forwardness, My Queen," said the girl, panting. She fell to one knee.

Channary sneered, disgusted. "How dare you approach me in such an informal manner? I will have you flogged for your disrespect."

The girl shuddered. "I-I do apologize," she stammered, as if she hadn't been heard the first time. "I was sent by Dr. O'Connor from the AR-C med-center with an urgent message for—"

"Did I ask who sent you?" said Channary. "Did I suggest

in any way that I cared where you were sent from or whether you had a message or who that message might be for? No, because I do not have the time to listen to every person who would seek an audience with me. There is a method to having your voice heard. Guards, escort this woman away."

The girl's eyes widened. "But—"

"Oh, stars above, I'll handle her request," said Levana. "Go to your fitting, as it is clearly more important than listening to a message from a girl who has run herself ragged trying to get here."

Channary snarled. "You will not speak disrespectfully to me in front of one of my subjects."

Levana flattened her hands against her skirt, to keep them from becoming fists. "I meant no disrespect, My Queen. Only that you seem to have a lot on your schedule today, so please, allow me to assist you with your royal duties." She nodded at the girl, who still remained on one knee. "What is your message?"

The girl gulped. "It is for a royal guard, Your Highness. Sir Evret Hayle. His wife has gone into labor. They fear ... the doctor ... they have requested that he come see her right away."

Levana felt a clamp tighten around her rib cage, forcing

all the air from her lungs. She glanced back in time to catch the dawning horror on Evret's face.

But then Channary started to laugh. "What a shame. Sir Hayle has only just begun his shift. His wife will have to wait until he is relieved. Come along, Levana." Gathering her skirt, she began marching up the steps.

Evret looked from the girl—a nurse, perhaps, or an assistant—to the queen's retreating back. He seemed cemented to the spot in the middle of the corridor. To leave would be to disobey a direct order from his sovereign. Such an act would mark him as a traitor, and result in what punishment Levana could only guess.

But his indecision did not wane. How desperate he must be to defy the queen.

On top of that, Levana's own curiosity was piqued. Babies were born all the time and complications were so rare, and yet, Solstice had seemed so weak . . .

Levana stepped forward. "Sister?"

Channary paused, nearly to the top of the stairs.

"I am going into town, and require an escort. I am taking Sir Hayle with me."

Her sister's face was murderous when she turned, but Levana lifted her head and fixed her own glare upon her. She would suffer the consequences later, and she knew very well there would be consequences. But she doubted that Channary would risk being defied in public a second time, and this way she alone would take the blame. Evret would only be following orders. *Her* orders.

The electrified moment stretched on for ages. Levana waited, and imagined that she could feel Evret's terrified heartbeat pounding into her, even from six paces away.

"Fine," Channary finally conceded, her voice nonchalant, and all the tension seemed to melt away from them. It was a false release, Levana knew. "If you happen to pass down Lake Boulevard, do bring me back some sour apple petites, won't you?"

With a flip of her hair, the queen turned away and continued up the stairs.

Peculiarly dizzy, Levana realized that she'd been holding her breath.

Only when Channary was no longer visible did Evret break from his watchful position. "My wife?" he said, emotion filling up his voice, his shoulders, his eyes. He walked right past Levana and grasped the nurse's elbows, lifting her to her feet. He seemed wary and anxious, almost as if he'd been expecting this. "Is she . . . ?"

Still pale from her encounter with the queen, the nurse took a moment to comprehend his question, before sympathy creased her brows. "We should hurry."

LEVANA WAS LEFT IN A WAITING ROOM WHILE THE NURSE escorted Evret down the sterile white hall of the med-center. She saw them pause at a doorway, and Evret's face was so contorted with worry that Levana wished she could wrap her arms around him and let all of his concerns soak into her. The nurse opened the door and even from this distance Levana caught a shrill scream before Evret disappeared inside and the door shut behind him.

His wife was dying.

The nurse hadn't said as much, but Levana knew it was true. It was clear that Evret had been hurried here because it would be his only chance to say good-bye, just as it was clear that it wasn't a complete surprise to him. Perhaps she'd been ill. Perhaps the pregnancy had already suffered complications.

Levana remembered seeing Solstice at the funeral. How she'd looked as breakable as a porcelain vase. The concern on Evret's face as they'd moved through the receiving line.

Levana took to pacing back and forth. A holograph node attached to the wall was broadcasting a silent drama in which all of the actors wore elaborate masks and costumes and twirled together in a graceful dance, oblivious to the empty chairs of the waiting room.

She did not leave the palace often, but now she found it refreshing to be where no one would recognize the glamour she'd been wearing since the coronation. The invisible girl, the unknown princess. She could have been anyone, for all the doctors and nurses knew. The medical center wasn't very big—sickness was rare in Artemisia, so mostly the clinic served for setting broken bones or easing some elderly patient into death or, of course, childbirth.

Despite being small, the clinic was busy, the staff constantly darting through the halls, emerging from and disappearing into countless doorways. But Levana could think only of Evret and what was happening behind that closed door.

His wife was dying.

He would be alone.

Levana knew it was so very wrong to think, but she couldn't fully deny the spark that flared behind her sternum.

This was fate.

This was meant to be.

His kind words at the funeral. His bashful glance during her birthday celebration. The little Earth charm. *Your friend, and most loyal servant.*

Was there meaning behind the words, something he couldn't say before now? Could he possibly want her as much as she wanted him?

Evret seemed like the type that would never disregard his vows of matrimony, no matter how much he yearned for another. And now he wouldn't have to. He could be hers.

Thinking of it made her whole body shiver with anticipation.

How long would he wait to make his intentions known? How long would he mourn the loss of his wife before he gave himself permission to declare himself to Levana, his princess?

Waiting would be agony. She would have to let him know that it was all right for him to mourn and love at the same time. She would not judge him, not when they were so clearly destined for each other.

Fate was taking his wife away. It was as if the stars themselves were blessing their union.

The door opened down the hallway.

Without waiting for an invitation, Levana hurried forward, concern and curiosity pulsing through her veins. Just before she came to stand in the doorway, a cart was wheeled through it and she jumped back to keep the corner from jabbing her in the stomach.

Plastering her back to the wall, Levana saw that it was not just any medical cart, but one that held a tiny suspended-animation tank. The baby lying on the blue, squishy surface was screeching and fussing, small hands and wrinkled fingers flailing beside its head. Its eyes were not yet open.

Levana had the sudden, encompassing instinct to touch the child. To run her finger along those tiny knuckles. To stroke the short tufts of black hair sprouting from that tender scalp.

But then it was gone, wheeled fervently down the corridor.

Levana turned back toward the doorway. As the door slipped shut, she saw Evret in his guard uniform, hunched over his wife. A white blanket. Blood on the sheets. A sob.

The door closed.

The sound of Evret's sob continued on in Levana's ears, bouncing around inside her skull. Again and again and again.

AN HOUR PASSED. SHE SPENT MORE TIME IN THE WAITING room. Grew bored. Passed by the closed door separating her from Evret a dozen times, but he never emerged. She began to grow hungry, and realized that all she would have to do is tell one person her identity and demand they bring her something to eat, and any person in this building would fall over themselves to fulfill her wishes. The knowing of it made her want it less, and she forced herself to ignore the gnawing at her stomach.

Finally, she took to wandering the hallways, pressing herself to the sides when people marched past, focused and determined. She found the infant viewing room easy enough and slipped inside to stare at the new arrivals through a pane of glass. A nurse was on the other side, administering drugs and checking vital signs.

She found Evret's child. A label was now printed on the side of the tank.

Hayle

3 January 109 T.E., 12:27 U.T.C.

Gender: F

Weight: 3.1 kg

Length: 48.7 cm

So he had a little girl. Her skin was dark like her father's, her cheeks as round and touchable as a cherub, and tufts of hair were just long enough to frizz out like a halo around her head, especially now that she had been cleaned. She was no longer fussing, just lay there in perfect peace, her little chest rising with each breath. She was impossibly small. Frighteningly delicate.

Levana had not seen many babies, but she could imagine that this was the most perfect child that had ever been born.

The little girl was the only one in the infant viewing room with a blanket wrapped around her that wasn't in plain hospital blue. Instead, the soft cotton material had been hand embroidered—a dozen different shades of white and gold creating a shimmering landscape around the child's tiny form. At first Levana thought it was meant to be the wild, desolate surface of Luna outside of the biodomes, but then she noticed the black trunks of leafless trees and, somewhere near the baby's ankles, stark red mittens lying abandoned in the snow, the likes of which Levana had only seen in children's stories. This was a scene from Earth, from a dark and cold season that Luna never experienced. She wondered what had even made Solstice think of it.

For this was so clearly the work of Solstice Hayle.

Listing her head, Levana let herself imagine that this baby was hers. That *she* had been the one to spend countless loving hours creating that illusion on the fabric. She wondered what it would be like to be a proud and exhausted mother, loving and adoring, looking down on the healthy little girl she'd given birth to.

Her glamour changed almost without her realizing it. Solstice Hayle. Beloved wife. Delighted mother. This time Levana kept her stomach flat and her figure lithe. She pressed a finger against the glass, tracing the outline of the child's face on the other side.

Then she spotted a shadow. Her own shadow on the glass. Her own reflection.

Levana flinched and the glamour disintegrated. She spun away, covering her face with both hands.

It took her a long while to shove the image from her thoughts. To call up the glamour of pale skin, waxen hair, frosty blue eyes.

"You can view her from here," said a voice from the hallway.

Levana's head snapped up as Evret was led into the viewing room. He looked as though he had just woken from a haunting dream. His eyes were rimmed in red when they fell on her and he spent a moment blinking. As if he couldn't see her, or couldn't place where he knew her from.

Levana gulped.

Recognition crept into his eyes and he bowed his head. "Your Highness. I didn't realize you would still be here . . ." His jaw worked for a moment. "But of course, you must require an escort. I am . . . I am so sorry to have kept you waiting."

"Not at all," she said. "I could have called for . . ."

But he was not looking at her anymore. His attention had drifted to the window and latched on to his baby girl.

Fathomless emotion misted over his gaze as he placed his fingers against the sill.

Then, between the heartbreak and the loneliness, there was love. So open and intense it stole Levana's breath away.

What she wouldn't give to be looked at like that.

"They tell me she's going to be all right," he said.

Levana kept her back against the window, afraid to catch her reflection and lose control of her glamour again. Afraid that if Evret saw her as she truly was, he wouldn't want her anymore.

"She's beautiful," she said.

"She's perfect," he murmured.

Levana dared to fixate on his profile. The fullness of his lips, the slope of his brow. "She looks like you."

He didn't respond for a long time. Just stared at his little girl while Levana stared at him. Finally, he said, "I think she'll have her mother in her, when she gets older." He paused, and Levana saw the strain of his Adam's apple in his throat. "Her mother—" He couldn't finish. He brought his hands up to his mouth, fingers laced together. "I would give anything . . ." He pressed his forehead against the glass. "She'll grow up without a mother. It isn't right."

Levana felt her heart stretching, like it was reaching out for him, trying desperately to connect. "Don't say that," she whispered, placing a hesitant hand on Evret's arm, and glad when he didn't pull away. "These things happen for a reason, don't they? Look at the child she gave you. She served her purpose."

Levana recognized the callousness of the statement at the same moment Evret jerked away from her. He turned to face her, shocked, and instant shame crawled down Levana's skin.

"That isn't . . . I didn't mean it like that. Only that . . . that you and this child still have your whole lives ahead of you. I know you must be hurting now, but don't give up hope on future happiness, and all the good things that are still to come for you."

He scrunched up his face, as if in physical pain, and it occurred to Levana that she was probably saying all the wrong things. She wanted to comfort him, but she couldn't imagine being devastated at the loss of someone. She had never felt that before.

Besides, the future was clear to her now, even if he couldn't see it through his sorrow. He would come to love *her*, Levana, once she was given the chance to make him happy.

"I commed a friend of mine, another guard—Garrison Clay. He and his wife are on their way here, to help"—he inhaled shakily—"to help with preparations, and . . . the baby . . ." He cleared his throat. "He can escort you back to the palace. I'm afraid I'll be no good to you in my current state, Your Highness."

Levana's shoulders fell. She had been filled up with fantasies of what could happen when Evret escorted her back, led her to her bedroom chambers, realized he was no longer required to be true to just one woman.

None of those fantasies had involved her leaving him here to weep.

"I can stay with you," she said. "I can comfort you. I can—"

"That is not your role, Your Highness, but thank you for your kindness. I would rather you had not seen me like this at all."

"Oh." She rolled the confession over in her thoughts, wondering if it was meant to be flattery.

"I haven't thanked you, for what you did today. With the queen. But you have my gratitude. I know it couldn't have been easy for you."

"Of course. I would do anything for you."

He looked at her, surprised, and bordering on alarmed. He hesitated, before turning away again. "You are gracious, Princess. But I'm only a guard. My place is to serve *you*."

"You are *not* only a guard. You are . . . you are perhaps my only friend."

He grimaced, which she couldn't understand.

Her voice dropped. "At least, you're the only person who gave me a birthday gift."

The look of pain turned to one of sympathy, and while his sorrowful gaze fixed on her again, she pulled the pendant from where it had been tucked beneath her dress's bodice. His sadness seemed to only increase when he saw it. "I have worn it every day since you gave it to me," she said, daring to speak over the yearning in her throat. "I value it above all the crown jewels, above . . . above anything on this moon."

With a heavy sigh, Evret took the charm and wrapped it up in Levana's fingers, then enclosed her hand in both of his. She felt dwarfed and delicate, like her heart was in her palm, not some vintage charm.

"You are a lovely girl," said Evret, "and you deserve the most priceless jewels that have ever adorned a princess. I'm honored that you consider me a friend."

She thought he would kiss her, but instead he pulled his hands away and turned back to the window.

Her heart was pattering now, and she knew her skin was flushed. She allowed some of the color to show through in her glamour. "I'm not like Channary. I don't want jewels. What I crave is much more precious than that." Levana inched toward him until her shoulder brushed against his arm. He shifted away, just barely.

He's in mourning, she reminded herself. *He's doing what he thinks is proper.*

But being proper seemed so very unimportant when her blood was simmering beneath her skin. When she felt like her heart would pound right through her rib cage if he didn't take her into his arms.

She ran her tongue along her lower lip, every sense heightened, and inched toward him again. "Sir Hayle... *Evret*..." The feel of his name on her lips, never whispered so intimately but in her fantasies, sent a chill down her spine.

But he backed away from her again, and his voice changed. More stern now. "I think it would be best for you to wait in the lobby, Your Highness."

His sudden coldness made her pause, and Levana slowly shrank back a step.

Mourning. He's in mourning.

She gulped, her dreams doused. "I'm sorry. I wasn't... I didn't mean... I can only imagine what you're going through..."

His expression softened, but he still didn't look at her. "I know. It's all right. I know you're only trying to help. But, please, Your Highness. I'd like to be alone right now."

"Of course. I understand." Although she didn't, not really.

She left him anyway, because he'd asked her to, and she would do anything for him. She may not understand his sorrow, but she *did* understand that Evret Hayle was a good man, and Solstice had been very, very lucky.

Soon, Levana told herself. Her life was changing, and soon perhaps she could be very, very lucky too.

SHE DREAMED OF HIM CONSTANTLY. HOLDING HER HAND in the dining hall while her sister prattled endlessly about the newest gowns she'd commissioned. Gazing at her lovingly across the throne room while the thaumaturges droned on about outdated policies that Channary would never bother to understand or improve. And every night he crawled into bed with her, wrapped her up in his muscular arms, breathed warm kisses against her neck.

A figment of him was with her when she woke up each morning.

A shadow of him followed her down every corridor.

Every time she caught sight of a guard's uniform from the corner of her eye, her heart ricocheted and her head twisted to see if it was him—though more often than not it was only her own stupid guards following respectfully in the distance.

Three days passed and his official time of mourning ended, but she did not see him.

Then a week.

It occurred to her that he may have taken leave from the palace to deal with his wife's death and spend time with his infant daughter, and she tried to be patient. To give him space and time. To wait until he came to her—because surely he would. Surely he missed her as much as she missed him.

She imagined him in his bed at night, all alone and dreaming about her in his arms.

She imagined him coming to her bedchambers, falling to his knees as he confessed how much he adored her, how he couldn't live another moment without knowing the taste of her lips.

She imagined them a happy family, her and Evret and the baby girl, playing make-believe together in the palace nurseries. She daydreamed about the plump little child crawling into her lap and falling asleep in her arms. She envisioned Evret's soft gaze upon them, knowing that his family was complete.

That they were meant to be together.

That she was the love of his life.

Another week passed, and still she had no word from him, not seen him at all. With every day, her yearning grew and grew.

Then, after an entire long day had come and gone, her fantasy came true.

A knock sounded at the door to her private chambers, and Sir Evret Hayle was announced.

Levana scampered out of the nook where she'd been watching a documentary about Luna's early colonization, shutting down the holograph node at the same time that she called up the glamour of the pale, invisible girl.

"Evret!" she cried, her heart thumping against her sternum.

He stepped back, startled, perhaps at her exuberance or the familiarity with which she used his name. He was holding a bundle of black-and-gold fabric in his arms.

Her two personal guards stood to either side of him, lacking any expression, as notable as statues.

"Your Highness," Evret said, bowing.

"Please, come in. It's—I'm so happy to see you. I've been thinking about you. Here, I'll call for some tea."

His brow was tense. He did not step past her threshold. "Thank you for your hospitality, Your Highness, but I'm to report for my return to active duty this afternoon. I only wanted to bring you this."

She hesitated. Return to active duty? So he had been on leave. She thought it might be a relief—part of her had been worried he might be intentionally avoiding her—and yet it was also irksome to think that he needed two entire weeks to mourn his wife, to attach to his daughter.

"Don't be silly," she said, pushing the door open more fully. "I will ensure that your tardiness is excused. Come in, just for a minute, please. I've mi—I've been worried about you. Wondering how you were."

Still he hesitated, glancing down at the fabric.

"Sir Hayle. Don't make me issue it as a command." She laughed, but his jaw only clenched in response. He did, however, step inside. His eyes darted around her chambers like he'd just entered a cage. She shut the door behind him.

Her palms were growing damp, her pulse humming. "Come in. Sit down. I didn't realize you were on leave. Though I'd been wondering . . ." She drifted into the parlor, and found that her legs were trembling by the time she lowered herself onto the cushioned divan. Evret did not come closer. Did not sit down.

She pretended not to notice his anxiety, but she *did* notice.

It made her own nervousness increase, memories of a thousand fantasies crushing down on her. Fantasies that had begun so much like this, only now it was real. He was *here*.

"Speak, Evret. Tell me what's become of you since we last saw each other."

He pulled himself up, like bracing himself for a blow. His

expression became stoic and professional, his gaze latching on the painting over Levana's shoulder.

"I was grateful to be given this time to make arrangements for my deceased wife, as I know you're aware, Your Highness, and also dealing with the effects of her business." His voice started to break, but he recovered smoothly. "I've spent this past week clearing her needlework shop and auctioning off what assets I could."

Levana's mouth pursed in a surprised O. She hadn't considered what might need to be done when someone died. After her parents' death, the thaumaturges and servants had dealt with everything.

"I . . . am sorry," she stammered, thinking it might be an appropriate thing to say. "I know you've been through a lot."

He nodded, as if to accept her compassion.

"And how is the child?"

"She is well, Your Highness, thank you." He sucked in a breath and held out the bundle in his arms. "I want you to have this."

"Thank you, Evret. What is it?"

Levana hoped that, by not moving from her spot on the divan, it would compel Evret to come closer. To sit beside her. To finally look her in the eyes.

Instead, he unfolded the fabric and spread it out,

revealing the elaborate quilt of Earth that Solstice had made, half of it pooling past his feet.

Levana gasped. It was every bit as striking as she remembered—even more so when surrounded by the luxuriousness of her royal chambers.

"Sol made it," Evret said, his voice heavy, "but I think you know that already."

Levana scanned the shimmering, patched-together pieces of Earth, up and up, until she was looking at Evret again. "It's magnificent. But why are you giving it to me?"

His face started to crumple, and he seemed to be holding his emotions together through stubborn determination. "She told me that you'd come into her shop, Your Highness. She said you admired it." He gulped. "I thought she would like for you to have it—as you were her princess, as you are mine. And I also thought . . . I wanted to show my gratitude to you, for persuading Her Majesty to let me go, when Sol was . . . You'll never know what that meant for me, Your Highness. You'll have my gratitude until the day I die."

Levana cleared her throat, eyeing the quilt. She loved everything about it—the design, the impeccable craftsmanship. She loved that Evret was giving it to *her*. But she also knew that she could never look on something that his wife had made and not feel a twinge of resentment.

"The quilt is extraordinary," she finally said, standing. "If it's all right with you, I'm going to store it somewhere safe, and we can give it to your daughter when she's older. She's the one that should have it."

Evret's eyes widened with surprise, then, slowly, softened into a hesitant smile. "I . . . thank you, Your Highness. That's . . ." He looked away, pressing his lips tight with emotion. "That is incredibly kind. *You* are incredibly kind. Thank you."

She shook her head. "You don't have to thank me. I don't want your gratitude, Evret."

He let his arms relax too, letting the quilt sag in front of him. "My friendship, then," he said. "If you still want it. Though I'm merely a guard, and not deserving of such a friend."

His smile was so unnerving that Levana had to turn away, flustered. She could feel her cheeks heating. Her heart was a volcano, now, hot lava gushing through her veins.

"No, Evret. You must know that I think of you as more than . . . than simply a friend."

The grin froze. His brow twitched with a hint of panic. "Your Highness—I . . ." He shook his head. "I didn't want my coming here to . . ."

"To what?" she urged, taking a step toward him.

"To give the wrong impression," he said, softening the words with another tentative smile. "You're a sweet girl.

Sometimes I think that you're . . . you're confused, but I know you mean well. And I know you're lonely. I see how you are around the rest of the court."

Levana bristled, mortified to think of all he had seen. Channary's taunts, the court's laughter . . .

"I know you need a friend. I can help you. I can be there for you." Dropping one corner of the quilt, he dragged a hand down his face. "I'm sorry, this is coming out wrong. I didn't mean that to sound so . . ."

"Condescending?"

He flinched. "I *care* about you. That's what I'm trying to say. I'm here for you, if you ever need someone to talk to, someone you can be yourself around."

Levana bit her lower lip, irritated, but also filled with such adoration for this man that she wanted to weep. Her gaze traced the continents of Earth, the patchwork of raw edges and shimmering gold thread. She inhaled, deeply.

"I know," she said. "I know you care about me. You're the only one who does." Smiling bashfully, she dared to meet his eyes again. "First the pendant and now the quilt. It seems as though you're trying to give me the whole world, Sir Hayle."

He shook his head. "Only some kindness, Your Highness."

Her smile brightened as she stepped closer, her bare feet treading across the luxurious quilt, crossing over Antarctica, the Atlantic Ocean . . . "Are you sure?" she asked, imitating the seductive way she'd seen Channary look up through her lashes at a potential suitor. "Are you *sure* that's all you're here for, Sir Hayle?"

His attention had dropped to her feet crossing over the quilt. His brow furrowed. "Your Highness?"

"I'm not *confused*, Evret. I'm not *lonely*." She grasped the top edge of the quilt, and Evret let go. She let it fall to the ground, and his alarmed expression returned.

Evret stepped back, but without even realizing she was doing it, Levana reached out with her gift, subtly holding his feet in place. "Wha—?"

"I'm in love with you, Evret."

The concern deepened, a hundredfold. "Your Highness—no, that's not—"

"I know. I *know*. You were happily married. You loved your wife very much. I get it. But she's gone now, and I'm here, and don't you see? This was how it was meant to happen. This was always how it was meant to happen."

His mouth was hanging open now, staring at her as if he didn't recognize her. As if he hadn't been smiling so sweetly at her a moment before, saying all those endearing things he'd said. As if he hadn't already confessed the truth.

Friendship. *Friendship.*

No. The pendant, the quilt, his being here all alone in her chambers.

This was not a man who wanted to be friends. He was hers, as much as she was his.

He held up his hands to block her as she inched forward again. "Stop this," he hissed, keeping his voice low, as if worried that the guards outside the door might hear, might interrupt. "This is what I was afraid of. I know that you have"—he struggled for a moment to find a word—"*feelings* for me, Your Highness, and I am flattered, but I'm trying to—"

"I could be her, you know," Levana interrupted. "If that makes it easier for you."

His brow twitched, dismayed. "*What?*"

"I'm very good at it. You saw . . . you saw how convincing I can be."

"What are you—"

The glamour of Solstice Hayle came easier this time, a little bit easier every time. Levana was sure she'd committed the woman to memory, from the slender arch of her eyebrows to the subtle curl at the end of her long, dark hair.

Evret recoiled from her, though his feet remained bolted to the floor. "Princess. Stop it."

"But this is what you want, isn't it? This way you can have both. I'll be your wife. I'll be the mother of your child. Pretty soon people will forget all about the one that died, it will just be me and you and our perfect family, and you'll be a *prince*,

Evret, which will be so much better than being a guard and—"

"*Stop it!*"

She froze, the fire in her veins doused with the anger in his tone. His breath had become ragged and he was leaning so far away from her she worried he would fall over. Scowling, Levana released the power she held over his feet and he stumbled back until he was pressing against a wall.

"Please," he said. "Please go back to how you were. You don't understand . . . you don't know how you're hurting me."

Embarrassment wound its way up Levana's throat, coupled with determination that was just as strong. She stepped closer, almost touching him. Evret tried to shrink away, but he had nowhere to go.

"You can't tell me that you don't want me. After the birthday gift, and the card. After . . . every time you've smiled at me, and . . . "

"Good stars, Princess, I've been trying to be *nice*."

"You love me! Don't deny it."

"You're a child."

She ground her teeth, dizzy with wanting. "I'm a woman, as much as Solstice was. I'm almost the same age as my mother when she was married."

"Don't. *Don't*." His eyes were sparking now. Anger, maybe. Or passion.

She looked down at his clenched hands, imagined them on her waist, pulling her closer. "I know I'm right. You don't have to deny it anymore."

"No! You're *wrong*. I love my wife, and though you may look like her right now, you are *not* her." He turned his face away, cringing from his own words. "The last time I was in this palace I disobeyed my queen, and now I've insulted my princess before I've even returned to my post. I can't . . ." He grimaced. "By my word, I will tender my resignation from the royal guard tonight, and plead the crown will be merciful."

Wetness was pooling in Levana's eyes, but she blinked it away. "*No*. Your resignation is refused, and I will tell Channary to refuse it as well."

He groaned. "Your Highness, please don't . . ."

"I won't let you. And I won't let you deny what I know in my heart to be true."

Levana had always been much more adept at using her glamour than at controlling a person's emotions. That sort of manipulation was a job better left to the thaumaturges, with all their training and skills.

But now she forced her way into Evret's thoughts as easily as plunging a finger into wet soil. Guards were always easily controlled—a security measure—and Evret was no different. His mind offered no resistance.

"You love me," she said. *Pleaded.* She pressed her body against his, feeling the warmth and the strength and the forcefulness of his hands suddenly gripping her upper arms. "You love me."

He turned his head away. She could see the struggle on his face, feel the resistance that he tried to throw up around his mind. Around his heart.

A pathetic attempt.

He couldn't resist her. She wouldn't allow it. Not now. Not when he was meant to be hers. When she knew he wanted this as much as she did, if only he would *see* it.

"You love me," she whispered, her voice softer this time. "We belong together. You and me. This is fate, Evret. *Fate.*"

"Princess—"

She filled his heart with desire, his body with longing, his mind with the same certainty that she felt. She poured all her own emotions into him, and felt his resistance crumble. He shuddered, overwhelmed with all the same feelings that overwhelmed *her.*

"Tell me I'm right. Tell me you love me."

"I . . . I love you." The words were barely a murmur, cracking with desperation, and his entire body sagged with their release. "*Sol . . .*"

The name sent a jolt of hatred through her, but was forgotten when Evret Hayle pulled her close and kissed her.

She gasped against his mouth, and he said it again, breathing the word into her.

Sol...

Then she was drowning. Drowning in sensation and heat and the rush of her own blood and yearning and want and he loved her...

He loved her.

He loved her.

... he loved her...

"THAT ONE'S BEING DIFFICULT," SAID CHANNARY, BOBBING her foot to the fast-paced orchestral piece and pulling a glossy red cherry between her teeth. Leaning over the railing, she tossed the stem over the balcony edge, letting it flutter down to the ballroom floor and become lost in the kaleidoscope of gowns and elaborate hairstyles.

Beside her, Levana did not lean or jog her foot or even attempt to discern which suitor her sister was referring to. Her attention was fixed on Evret, stone-still and imposing beside the ballroom staircase, in an identical uniform to every other guard, and yet looking somehow more like royalty than hired brawn.

His expression was composed and stern. He had not glanced at her once since the ball had begun.

"Oh, I see," said Channary, flicking her eyelashes in Levana's direction, then down at Evret. "Now that you have your own toy to play with, you won't bother listening to me rant about mine?"

"He isn't a toy."

"No? A puppet, then."

Levana clenched her fists at her sides. "He isn't a puppet, either."

Channary smirked. Turning away from the railing, she beckoned toward one of the servants. At their side in a moment, the servant dropped to one knee and held a tray up above his head so that Channary could inspect his offerings. A dozen cordial glasses were set into a spiral upon the tray, each containing a different colored beverage. Channary selected one that was bright orange and syrupy thick. "Stay there, in case I want another," she said, turning back to her sister. "If he isn't a toy or a puppet, then why in the name of Cyprus Blackburn have you spent the past month dressed up like his simpleton wife?"

Heat flooded Levana's cheeks, but her glamour didn't flicker. Always cool, always composed, always cheerful and delicate and lovely. That was how she remembered Solstice

Hayle, from their brief interactions. That was how she would have everyone see her now.

"The poor woman died in childbirth," said Levana. "I'm paying homage."

"You are playing with his head." A sly grin crept over Channary's face. "Which would make me rather proud if you'd set your sights a bit higher. A palace guard, honestly. Once you're done with him, perhaps you can make eyes at one of the gardeners."

Levana cut her gaze toward her sister. "You're quite the hypocrite. Just how many palace guards have kept *you* company over the years?"

"Oh, countless." Channary took a sip from her drink, and her cunning smile lingered when she lowered it and inspected the poppy-colored contents again. She gave it a discerning sniff. "But never at the detriment of having fun elsewhere. Ideally, a lady will have three toys at once. One to romance her, one to bed her, and one to adorn her with very expensive jewelry."

Levana's eye began to twitch. "You have never had Evret."

Laughing heartily, Channary set the barely touched drink back on the tray and selected an aquamarine choice dusted with something white and shimmery on top. The servant did not move. "That's true. Though I'm sure he would be much less problematic than Constable Dubrovsky." She sighed. "The minx."

Dubrovsky? Levana squinted down into the flurry of dancers. It took a while, but finally she spotted the constable dancing with a young gentleman whose name escaped her. One of the family heirs, she was sure.

"Perhaps the difficulty is in his personal preferences."

Channary flicked her fingers. "I've come to learn that he isn't particular. Except, evidently, he is not interested in his queen. I can't understand it. I've been throwing hints at him since last sunset."

Glancing down, Levana saw that the servant's arm was beginning to shake. The drinks in his cordial glasses were vibrating. She selected a beverage that looked like melted chocolate. "You may go."

Channary snatched up a daffodil-yellow liqueur before the servant could escape, holding both drinks in her hand as she leaned over the balcony rail. She trained her focus on the constable again. Not in a swoony or dreamy way, but as if she were analyzing a war strategy.

"If you want him so much," said Levana, "why don't you just brainwash him into wanting you? It would be much simpler."

"You say that as if you have experience in such matters."

Gut tightening, Levana couldn't keep her attention from

darting to Evret again. Stoic, statuesque Evret. Did his eyes ever follow her around a room like hers followed him? Did he ever sneak glimpses of her when she wasn't looking? If so, she had yet to catch him in it, not once since their first kiss in her chambers.

"Manipulating your prey is an easy way to cheat at the game," said Channary. She dipped her tongue into the blue glass, coating it with silvery powder, and swallowed. Her expression became surprisingly pleased. "But I don't want to win that way. I will win when I go into Lunar history as the most desirable queen to ever walk these hallways."

"The most undiscerning queen, anyway. Don't you ever want to just . . . fall in love?"

"*Love.* What a child you are." With no apparent premeditation, Channary downed both of her drinks in two successive gulps. She balked at the combined taste, then started to laugh. "Love!" she screamed out into the dance floor, so loud that a few of the musicians startled and the music blustered momentarily before picking up again. "Love is a conquest! Love is a war!" A few people down below had stopped dancing to gawk at their mad queen. Levana shrank away from her. "Here is what I think of love!"

Channary threw her empty glasses down into the throngs, as hard as she could. One of them shattered on the polished floor. The other hit Constable Dubrovsky's partner in the eye. He yelped and held up his hands, too late.

A spiteful giggle rose up inside Channary and was just as quickly smothered by a dainty hand pressed over her mouth. "Oops!" she chirped, then laughed in earnest and pushed herself away from the railing. Aghast, Levana trailed after her. They ignored the guests who dropped into bows and curtsies as they passed. The queen looked positively fanatical with her laughter.

"And you think that's going to endear your constable to you?" said Levana, abandoning her own untouched drink on a sideboard. "Assaulting his dance partners?"

"It can't be any more absurd than your tactic." Channary rounded on her, bringing them to a sudden stop on the winding ramp that swirled around the ballroom, connecting the main floor to the first balcony. "Do you really think that by changing your glamour to look like his dead wife and manipulating him a couple of times a day, you're going to make him fall in love with you?"

Levana bristled. "I don't need to do anything. He's already in love with me. And I love him. But I suppose you wouldn't understand."

Smirking, Channary ducked her head closer and lowered her voice. "If you truly believe that he loves you, then why manipulate him at all? Why not let him keep his own emotions, unmolested? In fact, why not show him what you truly look like?" She snorted. "Or are you too afraid he'll run screaming from the room if you do that?"

Rage burst inside Levana's head. She was suddenly trembling—and even her glamour was showing the anger. It had been a long time since she'd lost such control.

Breathing slowly, she forced herself to relax. Her sister insulted others so that she could lift herself up in comparison. She was to be pitied, if anything.

"He is still in mourning," Levana said, pacing her words. "Because I love him, I am trying to make this transition as easy on him as possible."

Eyes twinkling, Channary listed her head to one side. "Oh, yes. We can *all* see how easy you're making this transition for him."

Levana lifted her chin. "I don't care what you think. I'm going to marry him. When he's ready, I'm going to marry him."

Channary raised a hand and patted Levana on the cheek. Though it was a gentle touch, Levana still recoiled from the gesture. "Then you are an even bigger idiot than I realized, baby sister." Dropping her hand, she strategically lowered the straps of her dress and strolled past Levana toward the dance floor.

Levana shut her eyes, trying to drown out the music that crashed and rolled against her, the mocking laughter of the guests, her sister's taunting words. Channary didn't understand. Levana wasn't only trying to replace Evret's dead wife, she was going to show him that she was the better choice to begin with. She would be more loving, more dedicated, more enigmatic. She would make him forget that he had ever had another lover at all.

But her stomach was still in chains when she opened her eyes and glanced toward the dance floor. At all the beautiful girls and beautiful boys in their beautiful clothes and their beautiful glamours. Perhaps it was not enough to take on the glamour of Evret's wife. Not if she was going to be better than her in every way.

She slinked backward, drawing away from the twirling, writhing crowd, until her back collided with a wall. A tapestry swayed against her shoulder. A glowing orb over her head gave a faint halo to the few couples that were loitering on the ramp.

She thought of Solstice, the woman he had loved so very much.

Levana decided that her hair would be just a bit glossier, and added a hint of red on a whim—for contrast, for allure. Her eyes would be larger, with more depth of color. Her lashes thicker and her complexion shimmering and flawless.

Her bust would be a little fuller and her waist a little trimmer and her lips would be a little . . . no, not a little. Her lips would be strikingly, vividly red.

When Evret looked at her, he would see perfection.

When *any* man looked at her, he would see perfection.

Maybe her sister was right. Maybe she truly was hideous. But so long as she could deceive everyone, what did it matter? She would make even that constable want her if she chose to.

She waited until the glamour had fully pieced together. These visions were what she was good at. The ability to make her glamour so real that she had no use of her true skin anymore.

Confident once more, she glided down to the base of the ramp. A few heads swiveled toward her as she floated among the dancers. She did not head straight for Evret, but rather curtsied and smiled at the nobles who sent her curious glances, making a slow but steady trail through the ballroom.

Even so, she was almost close enough to touch him before his absent gaze locked on to hers. For a moment he seemed to peer right through her. Then there was bewilderment, as his dark eyes scooped down her body before latching on to her face again.

Then, a strange mixture. Desire, she was sure of it—but also, perhaps, fear?

She did not know what to make of that.

"Sir Hayle," she said, and in that moment, she made the lightning choice to even improve upon her voice. *Like a lullaby,* she thought. *I will speak like whimsical birdsong.* "I would like to take a stroll by the lake. Will you accompany me?"

He wrestled with the request for all of two heartbeats, before dropping his head in a silent nod.

His station commanded that he follow at a respectful distance behind her as they traversed through the palace corridors and emerged onto the stone portico that divided the palace from the gardens and lakeshore. Artemisia Lake glinted in the darkness, reflecting the lights of the palace back up to the sky, along with an entire ocean's worth of stars. Levana had often imagined that she could dive into the water and find herself floating in space.

"When I was a child, I believed there would come a time when I would enjoy these parties," she said, trusting that Evret was listening although he walked some paces behind her. "But now I can see that they will never grow any less tiresome. Political dalliances, all under the guise of innocent amusement."

She smiled to herself, pleased with how wise and mature her words sounded. She felt more self-assured with her improved glamour than she had in months. Maybe her whole life.

"I would much rather be out here, enjoying such a pristine evening." She turned back. Evret lingered a dozen paces away, his face cast in shadow. "Wouldn't you?"

"*Princess.*" The word sent a shiver down her spine, for it was full of everything she'd seen in his eyes in the ballroom. Bewilderment and desire and fear.

"Why do you stand so far away, Sir Hayle?"

"I can protect you well enough from here, Your Highness."

"Can you? And what if an assassin were to fire a shot into my heart from one of those windows? Would you manage to get to me in time?"

"It is not an assassin I fear you need protection from."

She reached for the chain around her neck. "Then what do I need protection from?" She took a hesitant step toward him.

"Yourself," he said firmly. Then he stepped back and said, with much less conviction, "Or me, if you come any closer."

She paused. There was something different about him tonight, a strange reaction to her glamour. She wasn't sure if this was what she'd hoped for or not. Since the day he'd come to her chambers they had shared a hundred stolen moments. A brush of skin outside the dining hall. A possessive hand on her waist as she disappeared into her bedchambers for the night. A hasty, desperate kiss in the servants' halls before the changing of the guard.

But Levana was not so naïve as to pretend that every moment hadn't required mental pressure from her. Reshaping his thoughts to match her own, forcing her own desire upon him, reminding him again and again that he loved her. *He* loved *her*.

And six times—*six* times—he had broken the guard's code of conduct, the rule that he was not to speak unless one of his superiors bid him, to tell her that this had to stop. He had told her that he was confused and heartbroken and he couldn't imagine what had come over him and he hadn't meant to take advantage of her and he didn't blame her at all but they had to stop, they had to stop . . . until he was kissing her again.

So far, tonight, Levana had not had to manipulate his emotions. So far, it was only her glamour that had cajoled him.

"What do you mean, I need protection from you?"

"Your Highness." The fear faded away. Now he looked only tired. "Why are you torturing me like this?"

She drew back. "*Torturing* you?"

"Every time I'm away from you—when I'm off duty, taking care of my baby girl, my thoughts are solid. I know myself. I know my heart. I know that my wife is dead, but she gave me a beautiful gift before she left, and I'm thankful for that." He gulped. "I know that I am loyal to the crown, and I will serve faithfully as long as I can. And I know that I care for you, as . . . as a guard must care for his princess. And as a friend, I suppose."

"You are my—"

"But when you're near," he continued, and the interruption shocked Levana more than anything else that night. A guard never interrupted a member of the aristocracy, and certainly never a member of the royal family. " . . . my thoughts get all messed up again. You look like Solstice, and I get confused. My heart pounds so fast around you, but not in a happy way or a loving way. It's as though my body belongs to someone else and I can't keep my hands off you, even though I know how wrong it is. Stars above, I could be executed for this!"

"No! No, I would never let that happen to you."

"But you're the one *doing* this to me."

She froze.

"Aren't you?" he whispered. "This is all a manipulation. A trick played on the poor, weak-minded guard."

Levana shook her head and scrambled closer to him, pulling his hands into hers. "I don't think of you like that at all."

"Then why are you doing this?"

"Because I love you! And you love me, but you're too honorable to—"

"I *don't* love you!" he screamed, and the words struck her like a thousand shards of ice. "Or at least . . . I don't think I do. But you've got my mind so turned around I can hardly tell what's real anymore."

She attempted a gentle smile. "Don't you see? That's what love is supposed to feel like. All these conflicting emotions and bouts of passion that you can hardly control, and this constant twisting feeling in your stomach like you can't decide if you want to run away from that person . . . or if you want to run away *with* them."

His face was tense, like he was trying to hash out his words before he yelled again.

"You're wrong, Princess. I don't know what you're describing, but it isn't love."

Tears pricked at her eyes. "When you said that I needed protection from you, I didn't think that you intended to break my heart. When I have given . . . when I would do *anything* for you, Evret."

Pulling away from her, he curled his fingers into his thick coils of hair. "That isn't my intention, Princess. I don't think you understand what you're doing, how wrong it is. But this can't continue. In the end, you'll grow tired of this charade, and I *will* be punished for taking advantage of you. Don't you see that?"

"I told you, I won't let that happen."

He dropped his hands. "And you think the queen will listen to you?"

"She'll have to. She herself has had countless affairs with royal guards."

"*She* is not sixteen years old!"

Levana wrapped her arms around herself like a shield. "You think I'm just a naïve child."

"Yes. Naïve and confused and lonely."

She forced herself to hold his gaze. "And what about beautiful?"

He flinched and looked away.

"You also find me beautiful, don't you? Irresistible, even?"

"Princess—"

"Answer me."

"I can't."

"Because I'm right."

He said nothing.

Levana swallowed. "Marry me, Evret."

His eyes snapped back toward her, horrified, but she plowed on. "Marry me and you will be a prince. She cannot touch you."

"No. *No.* Solstice . . . and my darling Winter . . ."

Her heart stuttered, and she was surprised at how quickly her jealousy returned, how much it hurt. "*Winter?* Who's Winter?"

He laughed without humor, pulling both hands down his face. "She's my *daughter.* You believe that you love me and yet you haven't even asked what I named my one-month-old child? Don't you see how insane that is?"

She gulped. *Winter. Solstice.* Though they did not have seasons on Luna, she knew enough of the Earthen calendar to be familiar with how the words fit together. She remembered, too, the little baby blanket, embroidered with a snowy scene.

He meant to never forget his wife. Not for as long as he lived.

"Winter," she said, wetting her lips. "Your daughter will be a princess, with all the riches and privileges afforded to a girl of her station. Don't you want that for her?"

"I want her to be surrounded by love and respect. Not . . . not whatever games the people in that ballroom come up with to entertain themselves. Not whatever it is you're trying to do to me."

Clenching her fists, Levana strode forward so that she had to tilt her head back to look at him. "Winter will have a mother, and you will have a wife. And I will love you both better than she ever could have."

Shaking with fury and determination, Levana marched around him, back toward the palace. It took him a long time, but upon realizing that the princess could not be left unprotected, he followed.

THE RESISTANCE STARTED TO LEAVE EVRET AFTER THAT, AND Levana hoped he was beginning to forget his wife. Or—not forget her—but forget that she was a different woman altogether. His eyes frequently took on a hollow stare when he was in her presence, and when other members of the court were nearby, he was as unreadable as some extinct first-era alphabet. He gave away nothing. He could have been a stranger.

Which she knew was wise of him. He'd been right before. If her sister wanted to accuse him of taking advantage of the princess, it would be in her right to do so. Levana wasn't worried about it, though. Channary had her own romantic conquests to worry about and, besides, she had been making eyes at older men since she was even younger than Levana was now.

No, she was not worried.

Especially in those moments when they were finally alone. Those borrowed spaces of time when he was hers, entirely hers. She began to loosen her mental grip of him, little by little, and to her relief and her joy, his response to her only became braver. His hands more possessive. His caresses more daring.

The first night they spent together, he whispered a single word into her hair.

"Sol..."

Simultaneously filled with pain and pleasure, joy and rage, Levana had grit her teeth and held him closer.

When the dome brightened over the white city the following morning, Levana let him sleep until the servant entered to bring her breakfast. Mortified and distraught, Evret lay in bed, frozen, while Levana ordered the servant to cut and butter her rolls. Slice her fruit. Prepare the tea that she had no intention of drinking.

When the servant had gone, Evret scrambled from the sheets. She saw the moment when he took in the spots of blood on the white cotton. How quickly he turned away. How hastily he pulled on his clothes, muttering curses beneath his breath.

Sitting up against her feathered pillows, the tray settled across her lap, Levana dropped a berry onto her tongue. It was sour. Channary would have called for the servant to take it back, and the thought crossed her mind, but she buried it. She was not her sister.

"Not this," Evret said, without facing her. "I didn't think you would push it this far. I didn't think—" He fisted a hand into his hair, cursing again. "I'm so sorry, Princess."

She bristled, annoyed, but tried to play it off as a joke. "For leaving before breakfast?" Levana cooed. "I will have another tray sent for, if you're hungry."

"No. My daughter . . . she'll have been with the nanny all night. I hadn't planned on . . ."

Levana glared at his muscled back as he pulled his shirt over his head.

"I will pay for the nanny's additional time. Stay, Evret." She smoothed the blankets beside her.

He sat on the edge of the bed to pull on his shoes, shaking his head. Then, hesitating, he dropped the first shoe back to the floor. His shoulders slumped in defeat. Levana grinned as she sucked the berry juice left on her finger, and was preparing to scoot over, to make room for him against the headboard, when he started to speak, his voice thick with misery.

"I tried to leave. A week ago."

Levana hesitated, pulling her finger out of her mouth. "Leave?"

"We were packed and everything. I was going to take Winter to one of the lumber sectors, learn a new trade."

She squinted at the back of his head. "A new trade doing what? Toppling trees?"

"Maybe. Or at a lumber mill, or even making wood moldings, I don't know. I just wanted to be anywhere but here."

Aghast, she set the tray aside. "Then why didn't you? If you're so *desperate* to get away—"

"Her Majesty wouldn't allow it."

She froze.

"I gave her my resignation, and she laughed. She said she was having far too much fun watching you make a fool of yourself to let me go now. She even threatened to send guards after me and Winter if I dared to leave without her consent."

Levana shivered. "I don't care what she thinks."

"I do. She's my queen. She controls me as much as you do."

"I don't *control* you."

He looked at her, finally, but his expression was bewildered. "What do you think this is?"

"I'm—! I barely—!" She dug her nails into her palms. "You want me as much as I want you. I see it in your eyes every time you touch me."

He laughed, a cruel sound, so different from the warm, kind laughter she remembered. Gesturing at her face, he yelled, "You're wearing my wife's face! She was gone for two weeks and I was miserable and then she was back and I . . . but she's not back. It's you. It's just *you*, and you don't think that's manipulative?"

Shoving the blankets aside, Levana scrambled into the robe left on her vanity chair. "It's *my* face now. This is who *I* am, and you can't tell me that what happened last night was a mistake. That you didn't want it."

"I *never* wanted this." He massaged his brow. "The court is talking, and the other guards. The rumors about us—"

"What does that matter?" She choked down a calming breath. "I love you, Evret."

"You don't even know what that word means. I wish I could make you understand that." He gestured to the empty space between them. "Whatever this fantasy is that you've built in your head. None of it is real. You are not my wife and I...I need to go be with my daughter. The only part of her I have left."

Levana cinched the belt tight, then stood there, shaking with anger, as she watched him pull on his boots.

"You will marry me."

He paused briefly, before snapping the last buckle at the top of his boots. "Princess. Please. Not again."

"Tonight."

He stared at the floor for a long time. A painfully long time.

She didn't know what she expected to see when he finally lifted his head, but the nothingness surprised her.

They stared at each other for a painful, hollow moment, until it occurred to Levana that he had not said no.

She gulped, pressing forward. "I will find an officiant and we will meet in the sun chapel at nightfall."

His gaze again fell to the floor.

"Bring your daughter if you'd like. She should be there, I think. And the nanny to watch her." She pulled her hair over one shoulder, feeling better about their argument already. How many of his annoying points this would solve.

She would be his wife—he could no longer say that she wasn't.

She would be the mother to his child.

And the rumors would stop, for no one would dare speak ill of the princess's husband, the queen's brother-in-law.

"Well?" she said, daring him to say no. Already she was feeling for the energy that surrounded him, ready to bend him to her will if he denied her. This was for his own good. This was the only way to solidify their family. Their happiness.

Releasing the top of his boot, Evret slowly stood. His absent expression had turned sad.

Sad?

No, sympathetic. He felt sorry for her.

She frowned, casting a wall around her heart.

"You have a chance to find love, Princess. Real love. Don't throw that away on me. I beg you."

She crossed her arms over her chest. "I have already found love. I have shared my bed with him, and tonight, he will be my husband." She attempted a smile, but her confidence was waning. He had bruised it so many times, and she didn't want to face rejection now. She didn't want to force him into this.

But even as she thought it, she knew that she would, if that was the only way.

Evret pulled his weapon holster over his head, his knife hanging on one hip, his gun on the other. A guard. Her guard.

"Well?" Levana demanded.

"Do I have a choice?"

She sneered. "Of course you have a choice. It is yes or no." Levana ignored the twist in her stomach that told her she was lying. He would not say no, and it wouldn't matter.

But still, she was surprised at how vulnerable she felt as the seconds ticked past. He wouldn't say no. Would he? She held her breath and sent—just a subtle tenderness into his thoughts. Just a warm reminder that they were meant to be together, forever.

He shuddered, and she wondered if he knew she was doing it. She stopped, and watched his shoulders relax.

"Evret?" She hated the whine in her voice. "Marry me, Evret."

He did not meet her eyes again as he crossed to her bedroom door. "As it pleases you, Your Highness."

THE OFFICIANT WRAPPED THE GOLD RIBBON AROUND Levana's wrist, explaining the significance of their union, the magnitude of the occasion as he tied a knot. He then moved to Evret, taking a second ribbon from the dish on the altar and knotting it around Evret's wrist. Levana watched closely as the shimmering ribbon settled against his dark skin. His arm was so much broader than hers, making her bones seem bird-like in comparison.

"Knotting the two ribbons together," said the officiant, taking them into his fingers and tying them once, then twice, "symbolizes the unity of bride and groom into one being and one soul, on this, the twenty-seventh day of April in the 109th year of the third era."

Releasing the ribbons, he let the knot dangle between their arms.

Levana stared at the knot and tried to feel connected. Unified. Like her soul had just merged with Evret's.

But she felt only a yawning distance between them.

A black hole of silence. He had barely spoken since arriving at the chapel.

In the second pew, the baby began to mewl. Evret turned and, annoyed at the distraction, Levana followed the look. The nanny was shushing the child, bouncing the girl gently in her lap, and Levana recognized the embroidered blanket that the child had been swaddled in, the pale snowscape, the red mittens. Sol's handiwork. Her teeth ground against each other.

"You will be exchanging rings?" asked the officiant.

Levana turned back and realized that neither Evret nor the officiant were still paying the fussy child any attention.

Evret nodded, though the action was curt. Levana glanced at him from the corner of her eye, surprised. She had not brought a ring.

Turning, Evret held his palm out toward the only guests other than the nanny and little Winter. That guard friend of his, Garrison Clay, who was there with his wife—a plain girl with strawberry-blonde hair—and their own child. A tow-headed toddler boy who had spent the ceremony bobbling down the aisle while his mother hissed for him to come back, gave up, chased after him.

Although their presence seemed to indicate that Evret was taking this ceremony with some levity, Levana couldn't help but be annoyed at everything about this family.

When they had first arrived, Garrison had pulled Evret aside. They'd seemed to be arguing about something, and she was certain he'd been trying to persuade Evret not to go through with it.

The intrusion had not endeared the guard to Levana.

But now, he stepped forward without hesitation and pulled a hand from his pocket. In his palm rested two wedding bands, each carved of black regolith polished to a fine gleam. They were as simple as Levana had ever seen, and had never dreamed she would wear. A wedding band made for a guard's wife, not royalty.

Her heart snagged, her eyes misting.

It was perfect.

Garrison did not look at her as he put the rings into Evret's hand and returned to the pew beside his family.

"Please take hands and face each other for the exchange."

They turned, almost robotically. Levana inspected Evret's face, and his handsomeness warmed some of the chill from her bones. She tried to express, silently, how much she loved her ring. That it was everything she wanted. That *he* was everything she wanted.

His dark gaze settled on her.

She smiled, a little shy.

His inhale was sharp and he opened his mouth to speak. Hesitated. Shut it again.

Then he slid the ring onto her finger and repeated after the officiant. "With this ring, I take you, Princess Levana Blackburn of Luna, to be my wife. From this day forward, you will be my sun at dawn and my stars at night, and I vow to love and cherish you for all our days."

Her insides trembled, giddiness burbling through her. The smile came easier now as she stared down at the band on her finger and the slip of gold ribbon binding them together.

It had not seemed real that morning, that whole day, waiting to see if he would even come. And now it was happening. This was her wedding day. She was marrying Evret Hayle.

She didn't know if her body could contain the joy throbbing inside it as she took the second wedding band from Evret and went to slide it onto his finger.

She paused.

Another band was already there, nearly identical, and so dark it almost vanished into his skin.

She looked up. Evret's jaw was set.

"I will not take it off," he whispered, before she could gather her thoughts, "but I will wear both."

She looked at the ring again. Considered, for half a moment, forcing him to take off his old wedding band anyway.

But no—this was what he wanted. She would not take it from him.

"Of course," she whispered back, pushing the band onto his finger until she heard the quiet click of the two pieces of carved rock colliding.

"With this ring, I take you, Sir Evret Hayle of Luna, to be my husband. From this day forward, you will be my sun at dawn and my stars at night, and I vow to love and cherish you for all our days."

As the officiant confirmed the ceremony, baby Winter began to cry in earnest. Looking back, Levana saw that the toddler boy was hanging off the nanny's arms, trying to peer into the baby's swaddle.

Evret wrapped his hands around Levana's, regaining her attention. The kiss was a surprise. She hadn't heard the officiant order it. But it was a gentle kiss, perhaps the most gentle he'd ever given her, and it warmed her to her toes.

With that, the officiant untied the knotted ribbons, and Evret was hers.

"TELL ME IT ISN'T TRUE!" CHANNARY YELLED, STOMPING into Levana's dressing quarters the next day. Wearing little more than shredded ribbons that barely covered what a woman should have covered, Channary looked like an effervescent spirit beneath the glow of the chandeliers. A risqué effervescent spirit.

Levana dared not move as her seamstress whipped her needle and thread over the seam at Levana's waist, taking it in. She had made a comment about how Levana must not be eating well, how she needed to plump up a little to keep a good figure, like her older sister, and Levana forced her to hold her tongue after that. The seamstress flushed with embarrassment and returned silently to her work. It had since been a very long two hours.

She glanced at her fuming sister.

"Tell you what isn't true?"

"You idiot. Did you *marry* him?"

"Yes. As I told you I would."

Channary made a furious noise in the back of her throat. "Then you will have it annulled, and quickly, before the whole city finds out."

"I will not."

"Then I will have him executed."

Levana snarled. "No, you *won't*. Why do you even care? I love him. I chose him. It's done."

"So *love* him. Bed him if you like, but we do not marry *guards*." Channary gestured toward the wall—beyond it, the white city of Artemisia. "Do you know how many of the families I have promised your hand to, and Father before that? There are strategies in place. We need their support. We want them to feel invested in us as rulers, and for that we need to make alliances. That's how it works, Levana. That is your *only* role as a part of this family, and I will not have you ruining it."

"It's too late. I won't change it, and even if you did kill him, I would never marry to please you. I would rather die."

"That, too, can be arranged, baby sister."

The seamstress spooled out some more thread, kneeling by Levana's ankles. The woman wisely kept her eyes diverted and pretended not to be listening.

"Then you would have nothing to bargain with, so why bother?" Lifting her head, Levana forced a smile. "Besides, I have brought you a replacement princess to be wed off to whoever it pleases you. You'll just have to wait another sixteen years."

"Another princess?" Channary guffawed. "You mean that child? The baby of a guard and a seamstress? You think any one of the families will want *her*?"

"Of course. She is my child now, which means she is a princess, as sure as if I gave birth to her myself. By the time she's old enough, no one will even remember she had another mother, or that Evret had another wife."

"I suppose that's been your ingenious plan all along."

Staring at the wall, Levana said nothing.

"Have you even thought what you're going to do with the little brat?"

"What do you mean, what I'm going to do with her?"

"You don't actually intend to . . . *raise* her, I hope."

Dragging her gaze away from the wall, Levana peered down her nose toward her sister. "She will be raised as royalty. As we were."

"With nannies and tutors, ignored by her parents?"

"With everything she could *possibly* want. Every luxury, every toy. Besides." She lifted her hands to the side as the seamstress reached the seam beneath her underarm. "Evret loves her very much, as do I."

It was a lie, and she knew it was a lie. But she also felt that someday it could be true. The girl was her daughter now, after all, and she was a part of Evret, so how could Levana not love her?

Mostly, though, she said it just to watch the annoyance slip over her sister's face.

The seamstress finished the seam and Levana lowered her hands again, letting her fingers trail over the fine embroidery of the bodice. She felt peculiarly happy today, after spending her second night in a row curled against Evret's body. She was a wife, now. Though her dress did not bare half as much skin as her sister's, she felt much more the woman. She had what her sister did not have. A family. Someone to love her.

"I hope," Levana continued, more to herself now, "that little Princess Winter will soon have a brother or sister too."

Channary wheeled toward her. "You're already pregnant?"

"Not yet, no. But I don't see why it would take long."

She had been thinking about it a great deal, actually, often returning to the glamour of Solstice's pregnant belly when she was alone, running her fingers over the taut flesh. She had not really considered wanting a child until she had watched Evret holding his baby girl, seen the softness in his gaze. That was something she could give him too. Something that she could share with Solstice . . . no, Levana's child would be better than Solstice's, because hers would have royal blood.

Frowning, Channary crossed her arms beneath her breasts. "That will be one good thing to come out of this, then. When you have a child that is *actually* your own, then we'll discuss who best to marry them off to."

"How I do look forward to those conversations, sister."

"In the meantime," said Channary, "I am at least doing *my* duty to further our bloodline without tainting it with disgraceful marriages."

"What does that mean?"

Channary flipped her hair off her shoulder. "Little *Princess* Winter," she said mockingly, "will soon have a baby cousin."

Levana's jaw fell. Shoving the seamstress away, she gathered up her full skirt and stepped down from the pedestal. "You?" She glanced at Channary's belly, but it was as flat as ever. "For how long?"

"I'm not sure. I'll be seeing Dr. Eliot this afternoon." Glaring, she turned and headed back for the dressing room's doorway. "I hope it's a boy. I am so *sick* of stupid princesses."

"Wait—Channary!" She started to chase after her, a thousand questions in her head, but stopped when her sister wheeled back to face her, face drawn in agitation. "Whose is it? The Constable's?"

Channary scowled. "*Now* what are you talking about?"

"Constable Dubrovsky. Is he the father?"

Channary's face turned haughty. Reaching out, she grabbed ahold of the half-stitched panel of Levana's dress and ripped it down, revealing the scar tissue over Levana's ribs before she could think to glamour it into invisibility. Gasping, Levana drew away, scrambling to hold the material against her. "I have no idea who the father is," Channary snapped, turning away again. "Don't you see, Levana? That's the *point*."

SHE DID NOT BECOME PREGNANT, THOUGH SHE WENT TO
Evret's bedchambers nearly every night. He and Winter had
been moved into the royal family's private wing of the palace, but only a week went by before Levana decided it would
be safer to retire to her own room after her visits to him. She
was afraid of what might happen if he awoke before her one
morning and saw her without her glamour, and she was tired
of using her gift to drag him into a deep unconsciousness
every night.

It was not quite the marriage she'd dreamed of, but she
told herself it would get better. It would take time.

She did not come to love Princess Winter, who cried
every time Levana held her.

Evret refused to let anyone call him a prince, and even
vowed to keep his job as a palace guard, though Levana told
him over and over that it wasn't necessary. He was royalty
now; he never had to work again. This only seemed to irri-
tate him, though, so eventually Levana stopped pressing
the issue. Let him play guns and soldiers if it made him
happy.

Channary grew larger and they learned that the child
was not a boy. By that time, though, Channary didn't seem to
care. She glowed in a way that Levana knew pregnant women

were meant to, yet she hadn't imagined her sister would be the same way. She would let anyone touch her exposed belly, even the servants. Encouraged it, even. Would yell if a person didn't coo and aww and tell her what a beautiful mother she would make and how her daughter would surely grow up to be just like her, by all the lucky stars.

As the months passed, Levana came to feel like there must be some conspiracy against her. Rumors were spreading about any number of women in the court who were having babies. The whole city seemed suddenly full of their crying and howling. When Levana went to see Dr. Eliot for a private appointment to ask if there was something else she could be doing, she even learned that a pair of wedded royal scientists were pregnant—Dr. Darnel and his wife, both specialists on the genetic engineering team. The woman was more than three times Levana's age.

Dr. Eliot was largely unhelpful. She went on and on about how it could take time, and they would look into further treatment when Levana got a bit older, if they still had not had any success. The woman even had the nerve to tell Levana to *relax*, to not worry about it so much. It would happen when it was meant to happen.

Levana was tempted to make the infuriating woman jab a scalpel into her own eye.

Her sister. The old doctor. *Solstice.*

There could be nothing wrong with Evret.

So what was wrong with *her*?

Her only consolation was that, as a result of Channary's condition and her exuberant need to be coddled, the queen neglected her royal responsibilities more and more frequently. Days would pass without her showing up at court and Levana was sent to take her place in countless meetings. Though she needled her sister about it time and again, she didn't truly mind. She was fascinated by their politics and the inner workings of their system. She wanted to know everything, to claim what power she could scavenge, and her sister's absence gave her the perfect opportunity to do just that.

Then, on the twenty-first day of December in the 109th year of the third era, Queen Channary gave birth to a baby girl. She was officially named Princess Selene Channary Jannali Blackburn of Luna, but everything past Selene was immediately forgotten by everyone but the history texts. The celebrations throughout the city and even the outer sectors were riotous for a week.

The royal bloodline would continue.

The Lunar throne had an heir.

"I LIKE THE SILVER FOLIAGE. DON'T YOU AGREE, LITTLE sister?"

Levana tore her gaze away from the baby, who was laid out on an embroidered quilt in the center of the room as if this were a common day care and not a royal meeting to discuss the country's upcoming anniversary celebration. There were a number of designers, florists, decorators, bakers, caterers, and artisans standing against the room's back wall, each waiting to give their opinions and offer their expertise. It took a moment for Levana to realize her sister was asking about two enormous bouquets, almost identical but for some fuzzy silver leaves tucked into one, as opposed to more vibrant emerald green in the other.

"Silver," she said. "Yes. It's very nice."

"In fact, add more," said Channary, tapping a finger against her lips. "I want the whole room to sparkle. Is everyone listening?" Her voice rose. "Sparkle. Glitz. I want every surface to shimmer. I want every guest to be bedazzled. I want a reputation of throwing the best galas this city has ever seen. I want them to talk about it for *generations.* Is that understood?"

Nods of understanding were thrown around, but Channary had already stopped paying attention to them as she scanned the offerings before her. Platters of tiny desserts and cocktails with little ice cubes in them, each cube carved into the shape of the queen's crown.

"No, no, none of this is good enough." Channary grabbed a tray of hors d'oeuvres and tossed it against the wall. Everyone flinched. "I said I want it to sparkle—is that so hard to grasp? Are you all blind?"

No one pointed out that she had not told them this before. But of course, they should have known before coming to this meeting. Naturally.

Levana shook her head behind her sister's back.

The baby started crying.

Wheeling around, Channary tossed her arm toward Levana. "Take the child."

Levana blinked. "Me? Why me? Where's her nanny?"

"Oh, for star's sake, she only wants to be held." Channary started to cough. She turned hastily away, coughing into her elbow, as ladylike as she could. It seemed to Levana that she'd been coughing a lot lately—for weeks, if not months—and though Channary insisted it was only a temporary virus, it seemed to go on and on.

A servant rushed forward with a glass of water, but Channary grabbed it and threw *it* at the wall, too. Glass shattered across the stone as Channary stomped out of the room, still coughing.

The baby's screams grew more fervent. Levana approached her, hesitant.

Someone clapped. "Let's adjourn for today," said one of the event planners, ushering away the artisans. "Come back tomorrow with . . . your improved work."

Levana stood over the child for one dread-filled moment, watching at how her face reddened and pinched, at how her chubby arms writhed against the blanket. Her tufts of dark brown hair wisped in every direction.

Though the child was seven months old and hinting every day that she was about to start crawling, Levana could still count the times she'd held her niece on one hand. There was always someone else there to take the baby, and just like with Winter, this child did not seem to be warming up to her at all.

Huffing, she squared her shoulders and crouched down, scooping up the baby as gently as she could. Standing, she nestled the child in the crook of her arm and did her best to coo comforting words at her, but the crying went on and on, little fists thumping the air, beating against Levana's chest.

With an annoyed sigh, Levana paced back and forth through the room, before stepping out onto the balcony that overlooked Artemisia Lake. She could see members of the court milling about the lush palace gardens, a few of the aristocrats out in boats upon the lake's surface. In the sky, the Earth was nearly full. Huge and blue and white and stunning amid the starscape.

Once, she had persuaded Evret to go out on a boat with her, but he'd spent the whole time wishing he was back home with Winter, going on and on about how quickly she was growing, and speculating on what her first word might be.

That seemed like a long time ago.

In fact, it had been a long time since they'd done much of anything together.

Bouncing little Selene as gently as she could, Levana examined the face of her future queen. She wondered if this child would grow up to be as spoiled and ignorant as her mother, who cared more about the flower arrangements than political policy.

"I would be a better queen than your mother," she whispered. "I would be a better queen than you."

The baby continued to wail, spoiled and stupid.

There was no point thinking it, anyway. Channary was queen. Selene was the heir. Levana was just the princess, with a guard for a husband and a daughter without royal blood.

"I could drop you over this balcony, you know," she said, cooing the words softly. "You couldn't do anything about it."

The baby did not respond to the threat.

"I could *force* you to stop crying. Would you like that?"

It was a tempting thought, one that Levana barely managed to withstand. They were not supposed to manipulate young children, as studies suggested that too much tampering when they were so tiny and impressionable could disrupt the way their brains formed.

Levana was beginning to wonder how much damage just one little moment of silence could do . . . when she heard her sister's heels clapping across the meeting room's floor.

Turning, she saw that Channary was attempting to hide just how horrible a coughing attack it had been, storming back with a stick-straight spine and blazing eyes, her brown hair swinging against her shoulders. But her face was blotchy and a thin layer of sweat still clung to her upper lip.

She took the baby out of Levana's arms without preempt, without even a thank-you.

"Are you all right?" asked Levana. "You're not dying, are you?"

Shooting a glare at her, Channary turned away without taking even a moment to admire the view. As she paced back into the room, the child's crying began to subside, her pudgy fingers pawing at her mother's face.

It occurred to Levana that maybe babies weren't affected by glamours, and they all hated her because they could see what she was underneath.

"You've had that cough for a long time. Maybe you should see Dr. Eliot."

"Don't be ridiculous. I'm the queen," Channary said, as if this alone would protect her from illness. "Though, speaking of doctors, have you heard about that couple in bioengineering?" She grabbed a bottle from a satchel and fit it into the child's mouth. Levana was amazed every time she witnessed this motherly affection from her sister—a girl she had only ever known as cruel and selfish. Surely *their* mother never fed them. She wondered what possessed Channary to do it, when they had so many servants on hand.

"What doctors?"

"The ones that had the baby. Darnel, I think . . . the man is . . . heavens. Ancient. Sixty, maybe?"

Levana clenched her teeth. "I had heard they were expecting, yes."

"Well—they are finished expecting. The baby was a shell."

Eyes widening, Levana clasped a hand over her mouth. Pretending horror, but mostly to hide the bout of glee that threatened to spill out. "A shell?"

"Mm. A girl, I think. That thaumaturge went to collect her yesterday, for . . ." Channary sighed, like it was too exhausting to remember all these pesky details. "Whatever those scientists are using the shells for."

"Blood platelets. For an antidote to the disease."

"Yes, that's right. How can you remember all this?"

Frowning, Levana glanced down at the baby, who was now in a satiated stupor as she sucked on the bottle's nipple. She turned back to the view of Earth, of the lake, of all the happy couples.

"A shell," she murmured. "How *embarrassing.*"

"I've noticed that you're not getting any larger," said Channary, pacing out to join her on the balcony. "Unless your glamour is hiding it from us."

Setting her jaw, Levana didn't respond.

"Tell me, how is wedded bliss these days? It's been a while since I heard you wax on and on about how much you *love* your husband. I rather miss those days."

"We are fine, thank you," said Levana. Quickly realizing how very un-fine that sounded, she added, "I still love him very much. We're quite happy together."

Snorting, Channary leaned back against the rail. "Lies, lies. Though I can never tell whether you're lying to me or to yourself."

"I am not lying. He is everything I have ever wanted."

"How quaint. I really thought you would have set your sights a little . . . higher."

Channary's attention drifted upward, to the blue-and-white orb hanging in the sky.

"What does that mean?"

"Oh, I've been thinking more about Earthen politics, lately. Rather against my will, I admit. It's impossible not to when all the families go on and on about this biological warfare they're planning. It's exhausting."

"You are a model of patience," Levana deadpanned.

"Well, I've been seeing pictures of the royal family from the Eastern Commonwealth and . . . I'm rather intrigued." She tried to take the child's bottle away, but baby Selene whimpered and reached for it, pulling it back into her mouth.

"The royal family? Isn't the prince only a child?"

"A toddler, yes." Channary bent over her daughter, nestling the tufts of hair with her nose. "At first I thought, why, he might be a perfect little match for my perfect little girl." She lifted her gaze again. "But *then* I thought—why, I suppose I could marry too. And the emperor is quite handsome. Broad-shouldered. Always smartly dressed, though a little bland—Earthens, you know."

"Unfortunately, I do believe he is already married."

Channary snorted, and baby Selene finally released the bottle, finished. "Always the pessimist, baby sister. Perhaps he won't *always* be married." Shrugging, she lifted the baby over her shoulder to burp her, even though she had nothing to protect her fine gown. "It's just something I've been thinking about. I'm certainly not planning any assassination attempts *yet*, but ... well. I've heard Earth is nice this time of year."

"I think it is nice every time of year, depending on the hemisphere."

Channary quirked an eyebrow. "What is a hemisphere?"

Sighing, Levana shook her head. "Never mind. That baby is going to spit up all over your dress, you know."

"Oh, yes, I'm sick of this one. I'm sick of all of them, actually. Nothing in my whole wardrobe fits anymore, and I know it will just get worse if I end up pregnant again. It will be a full-time job for my seamstress. I've been thinking I might have her feet removed, so that she has nothing better to do." Her eyes sparkled, like it was a joke.

But Levana had seen that sparkle before. She was not so sure that Channary was joking.

QUEEN CHANNARY BLACKBURN OF LUNA DID NOT HAVE A chance to see to an assassination on the Earthen empress. She did not marry Emperor Rikan or see her child grow up to marry a prince.

Five months after their conversation, she did indeed have her seamstress's feet surgically removed, and the seamstress had not even recovered enough to get back to work before it was all for naught.

At the age of twenty-five, Queen Channary died from regolith poisoning in her lungs.

It was a disease that commonly afflicted those in the outer sectors, due to a lifetime spent breathing in the dust from Luna's caverns, but it was so unheard of among the aristocrats—and certainly among the royal family—that doctors had never even considered it a possibility, even when Channary broke down and talked to Dr. Eliot about her persistent cough.

The mystery was never solved, but Levana had a theory that her sister had been sneaking away to the regolith caves under the city for some of her romantic rendezvous.

The funeral was similar to that of their parents, and Levana's feelings were rather the same.

Princess Winter and Princess Selene attended, dressed in royal garb as befit their stature. Selene, now one year old, received kisses from a lot of strangers, but between the two, it was Winter who received the most compliments. She was indeed a very pretty child, and Evret was right—she was taking more after her mother every day.

Evret offered to work, guarding the queen's casket as it was carried through the streets on its way to be buried in a crater outside of the domes. Levana asked him not to. She'd hoped he would agree to stand by her side. To be her husband. But it didn't work. To him, duty came first.

The little boy who belonged to Sir Clay was there too, almost four years old now and pale blond as ever. He tried to teach the wobbly-footed girls how to play hide-and-seek among the pews, but they were still too young to understand.

Levana pretended to cry. She was assigned the role of queen regent until her niece's thirteenth birthday, at which time Selene would take her throne.

Twelve years.

Levana would be queen for twelve years.

She tried very, very hard not to smile until the funeral was over.

"HEAD THAUMATURGE HADDON IS RETIRING AT THE END of this month," said Venerable Annotel, keeping pace beside Levana as they made their way to the court meeting. "Have you considered who you might nominate for his replacement?"

"I've been thinking I would recommend Sybil Mira."

Annotel glanced sideways at her. "An *interesting* choice. Awfully young . . . The families thought you might be thinking of Thaumaturge Par—"

"Sybil has thus far excelled at the responsibilities given to her regarding gathering shell children."

"Oh, no doubt. She is very capable. But her inexperience—"

"And I believe that she earned a second-tier rank at only nineteen years old. The youngest in history. Isn't that true?"

"I . . . am not honestly sure."

"Well. I appreciate her ambition. She is motivated, and I like that. She reminds me of myself."

Annotel pursed his lips. He would be stuck now that Levana had made the comparison. "I am sure she is a wise choice," he said. "If this is your final decision, I think the families will approve."

"We will see. I have a month still to consider." She smiled, but then she spotted Evret down the hall. He was one of the guards waiting outside the conference room. Seeing him, she felt herself deflate. No matter how confident she became in her role of queen regent, every time her eyes fell on her husband, she felt like that same love-struck sixteen-year-old girl all over again.

She hoped to pass a smile his way, but Evret did not look at her as he and his comrade pulled open the doors.

Wetting her lips, Levana stepped inside.

As the doors shut, the family representatives stood. Levana approached the dais where the throne stood.

The queen's throne.

This room was among her favorites in the palace, and her appreciation for it had increased drastically the moment she'd first taken her seat in that magnificent chair. The room glinted and shimmered, all glass and white stone. From her position, she could see all of the members of the court seated around the intricately tiled floor, and directly opposite her was the magnificent view of Lake Artemisia and the white city.

Sitting there, Levana truly felt like the ruler of Luna.

"Be seated."

Chairs were still shuffling as she straightened her spine and gestured leisurely at Head Thaumaturge Haddon. "You may proceed."

"Thank you, Your Highness. I am pleased to report that your experiment regarding strict work hours in the outer sectors is going well."

"Oh?" Levana was not surprised, but she pretended that she was. She had read a study from Earth a few months ago about how efficiency and productivity dropped without regularly scheduled breaks. She suggested that they program chimes to sound at regular intervals in the manufacturing domes, to remind workers when to take mandatory breaks, and then extend the workday to cover that lost time. The court had not been sold on the strategy at first, worried that it would be too difficult to enforce such a drastic increase in the workday, and that there were already complaints of the people being overworked in the outer sectors. But Levana insisted that, with this new schedule, the days would in fact go *faster,* and the solution would benefit everyone, the workers most of all.

"Productivity is up eight percent in the three sectors where we implemented the change," Haddon continued, "with no apparent loss of quality."

"I am pleased to hear it."

Haddon read through the reports, feeding her the numbers on the successful increase of trade between sectors, and telling her how delighted the Artemisian families were with the new artisanal delights Levana had commissioned for their city. What's more, the research teams were making good progress with both the genetically engineered army and the biochemical disease, and reported that it might be ready to unleash on Earth within the next eighteen months.

No one came out and said it, but Levana could tell that the court was pleased with how she had stepped up to fill her sister's role, and far outdone the example that Channary, and even their parents, had set. She was the queen Luna had been waiting for, and since she had taken power, the city was thriving, the outer sectors were flourishing, everything was exactly as Levana knew it should be.

"We are planning to roll out the labor program through-out the rest of the general manufacturing sectors in the coming months," Haddon continued. "I will give regular up-dates as we progress. That said, I'm afraid we have noticed some . . . potential drawbacks."

Levana listed her head to one side. "And those would be?"

"With such frequent breaks during the workdays, the civilians are given more chances for socializing, and we've noticed that these interactions are continuing even after the workday has ended."

"And this is a problem?"

"Well . . . perhaps not, Your Highness."

Annotel spoke up. "In the past, there has been concern of civil unrest when the people spend too much time being idle and . . . having *ideas*."

Levana laughed. "Unrest? What reason would my people have to be unhappy?"

"None, of course, Your Highness," said Haddon. "But I wonder if we have yet fully recovered from the murders on your parents. It is only that there will always be a few . . . bad seeds, in the outer sectors. We would hate to give them too much time to infect the others."

Levana folded her hands in her lap. "While I cannot imagine the people deciding they're unhappy with our rule, I concede to your point. Why don't we implement a mandatory curfew after work hours? Give people time to go home, and let them stay there. That's the time to be with their families, anyway."

"Do we have the manpower to enforce that?" one of the nobles asked.

"Unlikely," said Haddon. "As a guess, we would need a forty percent increase in sector guards."

"Well then, hire more guards."

Looks were traded across the throne room, though no one argued the simplicity of this solution.

"Of course, My Queen. We will see that it is done."

"Good. You said there was another problem as well?"

"Not an immediate problem, but all of our projection reports show that this amount of production isn't sustainable in the long term. If we continue at these rates, we'll drain our resources. The available terra-formed land we have is already working at near-maximum capacity."

"Resources," Levana drawled. "You're telling me that we cannot continue to grow our economy because we are living on a *rock*."

"It is disheartening, but it is the truth. The only way to continue with this output is if we reopen trade agreements with Earth."

"Earth will not trade with us. Don't you understand that this is the entire point of developing the disease and antidote that we discuss at every meeting? Until we have that, then we have nothing to offer the Earthens that they do not already have."

"We have land, Your Highness."

Levana bristled. Though Haddon's voice didn't waver, she could see the hesitation in his eyes. With good reason.

"Land," she repeated.

"All of the sectors together still take up only a fraction of Luna's total surface. There is plenty of low-gravity real estate that could be quite valuable to Earthens. They could build spaceports that would require less fuel and energy to conduct their travel and exploration. That is what we could offer them. The same arrangement that the Lunar colony was first formed on."

"Absolutely not. I will not return us to the political strength of a colony. I will not be dependent on the Earthen Union."

"Your Highness—"

"The discussion is over. When you have another suggestion for how we can get around our dilemma of taxed resources, I will be open to hearing it. What next?"

The meeting continued amiably enough, but there was a tension in the court that never fully dissolved. Levana tried to ignore it.

She was the queen Luna had been waiting for. She would solve this problem too—for her people, for her country, for her throne.

"I'M TELLING YOU, I'M *GOOD* AT THIS," SAID LEVANA, PACING giddily around the bedroom.

"I'm sure you are," said Evret, laughing as Winter brought him a pair of Levana's shoes from the closet. "Thank you, darling," he said, setting the shoes aside. Winter gleefully darted back toward the closet. Looking up, Evret beamed. "This is the happiest I've seen you in a long time."

It was the happiest Levana had *felt* in a long time. "I've never been good at anything," she said. "Channary was the better dancer, the better singer, better at manipulation, better at everything. But *ha!* I am a better queen, and everyone knows it."

Evret's smile became hesitant, and she knew he was uncomfortable speaking ill of the dead, but Levana didn't care. It had been almost a year since Channary's death, and she'd felt like even a day of mourning was too much. She suspected that the poor seamstress who would never walk again would agree with her.

Winter scurried by, handing her father another pair of shoes. He patted her head, where her hair had grown into wild curls that haloed her round face. "Thank you."

She skipped away again.

"And the people. I think they're really starting to love me."

"*Love* you?"

Levana stopped pacing, caught off guard by the mocking in his tone.

Evret's smile quickly fell, as if he had caught the derision too late. "Sweetheart," he said, a name that he'd started using for her not long into their marriage. It simultaneously served to make her heart patter, and to make her question if he called her this so that he wouldn't accidentally call her *Solstice*. "You are no doubt a good queen, and doing great things for Artemisia. But the *people* don't know you. Have you even been to the outer sectors?"

"Of course I haven't. I'm the queen. I have people who go out there and report back."

"You're the queen regent," he corrected. Levana flinched— she was coming to despise the word *regent*. "And while I'm sure that the reports you get are very accurate, it still wouldn't allow for the people to get to know *you*, their ruler. They can't love a stranger. *Thank you*, Winter. And besides, whenever you do your news broadcasts, you always . . ."

She narrowed her eyes, waiting.

"It's just . . . you never show your face, when they record you. Rumors are starting, you know. People think you're hiding something. And love begins with trust, and trust can't be formed if people think you're hiding something."

"Glamours don't work through video. You know that. Everyone knows that."

"Then don't show them your glamour." He gestured at her face. "Why not just be yourself? They'll admire you for it."

"How would you know? You've never seen me!"

He was momentarily taken aback, his dark eyes blinking up at her. Winter, too, stopped in the doorway, carrying yet another pair of glittering shoes.

Evret stood and cleared his throat. "You're right, but whose fault is that?"

"Papa?" said Winter, cocking her head. "Why is Mother yelling?"

Levana rolled her eyes. This was how it had been since the day Winter started speaking. She addressed her father only. Levana was just the bystander, a *mother* in title only.

"No reason, darling. Why don't you go play with your dolls?" Nudging Winter toward the playroom, Evret poured himself a drink from a small tray on the side table. "You do realize that you have been my wife now for more than three years," he said, watching the amber liquid splash over the ice cubes. "I have not fought you. I have not left. But I'm beginning to wonder if this will ever become a real marriage, or if you plan on living this lie until one of us is dead."

Levana's diaphragm quivered unexpectedly, warning her that she might cry, telling her that his words hurt more than she admitted on the surface.

"You think our marriage is a lie?"

"As you just said—even *I* have never seen what you really look like."

"And that's what's important to you? That I be beautiful, like *she* was."

"Stars above, Levana." He pressed the glass onto the table without taking a drink. "*You're* the one who impersonates her. You're the one who hides. I've never wanted that. What exactly are you afraid of?"

"That you would never look at me again! Trust me, Evret. You would never see me the same way."

"You think I'm that shallow? That I care at all what you look like under your glamour?"

She turned away. "You don't know what you're asking."

"I think I do. I know—there are scars, burns of some sort. I've heard the rumors."

Levana grimaced.

"And I know your sister said you were ugly from the time

you were a baby, and I can only imagine the kind of damage that does to a person. But . . . Levana . . ." Sighing, Evret came up behind her, settling his warm hands on her shoulders. "I had a wife once that I could talk to about anything. That I trusted implicitly. I think, if you and I are going to make this work, we need to at least *try* to have that too. But that will never happen if you're always going to hide from me."

"That will never happen," Levana hissed, "if you constantly insist on comparing me with *her.*"

He turned her around to face him. "You compare yourself with her." He cupped her face. "Let me see you. Let me judge for myself what I can or can't handle." He gestured to the window. "Let the people judge for *themselves.*"

Levana gulped, afraid to realize that she was considering it.

Was it true, that he could never know her, trust her, *love* her, so long as she hid behind this glamour of beauty and perfection?

"No, I can't do it," she whispered, pulling herself out of his grip. His face fell, and a moment later his hands did too. "Maybe you're right about the people. No—you *are* right. I'll plan a tour through the outer sectors. I'll let them see me."

"Your glamour, you mean."

She grated her teeth. "*Me.* This is all that matters, so please, don't ask me again."

Shaking his head, he returned for his drink.

"Trust me," Levana said emphatically, even as her vision blurred. "It's better this way. *I'm* better this way."

"That's the problem," he said, unable to look at her as he took a sip. "I don't trust you. I don't even know how to start."

THE IDEA CAME TO HER SLOWLY. AT FIRST, IT WAS MERELY A horrible, guilty fantasy. That there was no Selene. That Channary had died, alone and childless. That Levana was already the true queen.

Then one day, as she was watching Winter and Selene playing with blocks on the floor of their nursery, babbling in a language only they understood, Levana had a fantasy of Selene dying.

Putting one of those blocks in her mouth and choking on it.

Slipping in the bathtub, and her nanny being too distracted to notice.

Tripping on her own uncertain feet and tumbling down the hard palace steps.

The daydreams disgusted her at first—all over an innocent child, with big brown eyes and messy brown hair too frequently left uncombed—but she told herself they were just that, daydreams. There was no harm in imagining some innocent mistake that would lead to the baby dying, and the country mourning, and Levana being crowned the queen, now and forever.

Over time, the fantasies became more violent.

In a frustrated fit, her nanny would throw Selene off the balcony.

Or, rather than tripping over her own feet, some jealous child from the aristocracy would push her down the stairs.

Or a disillusioned shell would sneak into the palace and stab her sixteen times in the chest.

Even as Levana became afraid to think that these were her own thoughts, she could hear herself justifying them.

She was a great queen. Luna was better off with her, not some ignorant child who would be a spoiled, self-absorbed brat by the time she took her throne.

The transition when Selene turned thirteen would be difficult and confusing for the people. It could take years for them to get on track again.

Channary had been a terrible ruler. No doubt her daughter would be the same.

No one would love this country like Levana did. *No one.*

She deserved to be the queen.

Because she had never truly hated the child, she believed she was being practical in her rationalization. Her thoughts didn't come from envy or resentment. This was about the good of Luna. The betterment of everyone around her.

Months ticked by, and she found herself inspecting the few moments she spent with her niece for weaknesses. Wondering how she would do it, if the opportunity came. Wondering if she could get away with it.

Levana didn't realize she was making a plan until the plan was already half formed.

It was the right thing to do. The only choice a concerned queen could make.

It was a sacrifice and a burden that she couldn't hand to anyone else.

She chose a day, almost without realizing she had chosen it.

The opportunity presented itself so clearly. Her imagination sparked. It was as though some unseen ghost was whispering the suggestion into her ear, coaxing her to take advantage of this chance that might not come again.

Winter had an appointment with Dr. Eliot that day. Levana would ensure that she was the one who would get Winter from the nursery. She would send Evret on some other task. The nanny would be there. Supposedly there was a new nanny, one that people didn't know well yet, one that may not be entirely trustworthy. Levana would coerce her, making sure it seemed like an accident. She would . . .

Would what?

This was the part that Levana could not figure out.

How did you kill a child?

There were so many possibilities, but every one of them made her feel like a monster for even considering it. At first she tried to think how best to make sure the child didn't suffer. She didn't want to cause her pain; she only wanted her dead. Something that would be over quickly.

Then, on Selene's third birthday, they decided to host a party. Something intimate. It had been Evret's idea, and Levana was so delighted to see him wanting to plan something, as a family, that she didn't argue. It was only the two of them, and little Winter, of course, and the Clay family, as always. All gathered together in the palace nursery, drinking wine and laughing like normal people, like there was nothing strange about this mingling of royalty and guards. The children played, and Garrison's wife gave Selene a stuffed doll that she'd made, and the palace pastry chef brought up a little cake shaped like a crown. In each of the cake's tines was a tiny silver candle.

Evret tried to show Selene how to blow out the candles, while wax dripped into the frosting. Winter, too, wanted to take part in the celebration, and baby spittle was left all over the pretty cake before young Jacin Clay got annoyed and blew out the candles himself. They all laughed and clapped, and Levana stared at the black smoke curling upward and knew how she was going to do it.

She would do to the child what Channary had done to her.

Come here, baby sister. I want to show you something.

Only, unlike Channary, *she* would be merciful. She would not force the child to then go on living.

SHE STOOD IN THE DOORWAY TO THE NURSERY, LISTENING to the girls giggling in their playhouse. They had covered the top with blankets from Evret's bed for added privacy. From here, Levana could see intricate apple blossoms embroidered around the edges of one of the blankets, and it surprised her to think that, no matter how many times she had slipped into Evret's bed, she had never noticed those designs. The blanket was not something commissioned for the palace, which meant that Evret had brought it from his previous marriage, and had kept this secret part of Solstice hidden these past years.

Realizing that she was fidgeting with her black wedding band, Levana let her hands fall to her sides.

Inside the playhouse, Winter said something about being princesses in the tower, but then it all dissolved into childish nonsense and laughter that Levana couldn't follow.

It would be over after today, and that knowledge was a relief. She could stop thinking about the princess that would one day grow up and take everything from her. She could stop being haunted by the ghost of her sister and the legacy she'd left behind.

After today, all of Luna would be hers.

It had occurred to her that she could choose not to take Winter away after all, and to let the fire claim them both. Then all of Evret would be hers too. But then she thought of what a hollowed-out shell of a man Evret had been in the months following his wife's death, and she couldn't stand to watch that again.

"Oh, pardon me. Are you—"

Levana turned and the girl drew back with a gasp, before falling into a hasty curtsy. "Forgive me, Your Majesty. I didn't recognize you."

The girl was no great beauty, with limp hair and a nose too large for her face. But there was a delicateness to her that Levana thought could appeal to some, and a grace in her curtsy that befit someone who had been hired to raise their next queen.

"You must be the new nanny," said Levana.

"Y-yes, My Queen. It is a great honor to be in your presence."

"I am not the queen," said Levana, tasting her own bitterness. "I am merely keeping watch over the throne until my niece is older."

"Oh, yes, of course. I...I meant no disrespect. Your... Highness."

The giggling had stopped. When Levana glanced toward the playhouse, she saw that the girls had pulled back the blankets and were watching with curious eyes and open mouths.

"Winter is being seen by Dr. Eliot today," said Levana. "I've come to take her."

The nanny stayed in her curtsy, uncertain if she was allowed to rise and look upon Levana or not. It was obvious from the stretched-thin silence that she wanted to ask why the queen would bother when it was within the nanny's own duties to make sure the girls made their appointments, or why the doctor didn't come see the princess here in the nursery. But she didn't argue. Of course she didn't.

"Winter, come along," Levana called. The blanket fell again, hiding the princesses. "You have an appointment with Dr. Eliot. Let's not keep her waiting."

"Shall I expect the princess's return this afternoon, Your Highness?" asked the nanny.

Levana's gut tightened. "No. I will take her back to our private quarters after the appointment." She watched as Winter climbed down the ladder, graceful in the way that only a four-year-old child could be, even with her chubby legs and a very full skirt. Her hair bounced as she dropped to the floor.

The blanket shifted again. Selene, peering out from the gap.

Levana met her stare, and she could sense the distrust from the child, the instinctual dislike. Jaw tightening, she sucked in a quick breath.

"I have a job for you."

The nanny, growing uncomfortable, rose from the curtsy. "For me, Your Highness?"

"Do you have a family? Any children of your own?"

"Oh. No, Your Highness."

"A husband, or a lover?"

The girl flushed. She was probably no more than fifteen herself, but that meant so little in Artemisia.

"No. I am not married, Your Highness."

Levana nodded. Selene had no family, and neither did this girl—none that needed her, at least. It was perfect.

It was meant to be.

A hand slipped into Levana's, making her jump.

"I'm ready to go, Mother," said Winter.

Pulse thrumming, Levana yanked her hand away. "Go wait in the corridor. I'll be there in a moment."

Crestfallen, Winter turned and waved at Selene. A tiny hand snaked out from beneath the blanket and waved back, before Winter floated out of the nursery.

Now. She would do it now.

After today, it would all be over.

Levana pressed her hands against her skirt, wicking off her damp palms. "Go into the playhouse," she said, almost like she was speaking to herself. "Go be with the princess. It is almost time for her nap." She spoke slowly, impressing the idea into the nanny's mind. Reaching into a hidden pocket, she produced a candle, already half burned. "It will be dark under that blanket, so you will want this candle to see by. Set it out of the way so the princess doesn't accidentally burn herself. Near the edge of the playhouse. Under that blanket...the one with the apple blossoms. You will stay with the girl until you both fall asleep. You are already tired. It will not take long."

The nanny tilted her head to one side, like listening to a song that she couldn't quite place.

Producing a tiny book of matches, Levana let the nanny hold the candle while she lit it. Her hands trembled with the spark of the match, fear of the flame tensing every muscle. By the time the wick took light, she could feel the flame creeping up the little match, threatening to singe her fingers.

Levana hastily shook it out, breathing easier the second the flame was extinguished. She dropped the smoldering match into the nanny's apron pocket. The girl said nothing.

"Go now. The princess is waiting."

Empty eyed, the nanny turned and wandered toward the little playhouse, carrying the lit candle aloft. Selene was peering out again. Confused and curious.

Licking her lips, Levana forced herself to turn away. In the corridor, she grabbed Winter's hand without a word and tugged her toward the doctor's office. Her heart was pummeling against the inside of her chest.

She had done it. She had done what she needed to do.

Now she had only to wait.

IT WAS MORE THAN AN HOUR BEFORE LEVANA HEARD THE first stirrings within the palace. Though her nerves were throbbing the entire time since she'd left the nursery, it had already begun to feel like a dream. Just another one of her fantasies, resulting in disappointment. While Dr. Eliot checked that Winter was as healthy as any child had ever been, Levana paced around the waiting room. The doctor's office was in the palace, a satellite office from the one she kept at the med-center on the other side of the city, so that she could be on call at the slightest sign of a cough or fever from the royal family.

Realizing that she was still holding the little book of matches, Levana checked that no one was around and dropped them into a trash bin, then wiped her hands on an upholstered chair as if the evidence might show itself in ashen traces on her fingertips.

"*Doctor!*"

Levana jumped, spinning toward the office's open doorway. In the other room, Dr. Eliot's voice went quiet, and then she appeared holding a vitals scanner in one hand. Behind her, Winter was sitting on a papered table, swinging her stockinged feet against the side.

A servant appeared, face red and panting for breath.

"*Doctor!* Come quick!"

"I beg your pardon, but I am with Her Highness and—"

"No—it's the nursery! *Princess Selene!*" The servant's voice pitched so high it cracked.

A chill rolled across Levana's skin, but she managed to maintain her baffled expression.

"Whatever could be—"

"There was a fire. Please, you have to come. There's no time to lose!"

Dr. Eliot hesitated, glancing at Levana, then back at Winter.

Gulping, Levana took a step forward. "Well, of course, you must go. If our future queen is in danger, you must see to her at once."

It was all the prompting the doctor needed. As she scooped up a medical bag, Levana turned to the servant. "What's happened? What about a fire?"

"We're not sure, Your Highness. They were in the playhouse and it caught fire . . . we think they must have been sleeping . . ."

"They?"

"The princess and her nanny." Gaze alighting on Winter, the servant suddenly started to sob. "Thank the stars Princess Winter wasn't there too. It's awful. *Awful!*"

It took only a few seconds for Levana to become annoyed with the servant's wails.

Winter hopped down from the table and went to put on her shoes, but Levana grabbed her wrist and dragged her after the doctor. "Not now, Winter. We'll come back for them."

The doctor ran. Levana wanted to. Her curiosity was

agony, all her fantasies accumulating in that breathless moment. But she didn't want to carry Winter, and princesses did not run.

Future queens did not run.

She was still gripping Winter's hand when she smelled the smoke. Heard the screams. Felt the pounding of footsteps reverberating through the floors.

A crowd had gathered by the time they arrived. Servants and guards and thaumaturges filling up the corridor.

"*WINTER!*" It was Evret, his face made of relief when he spotted his child. Shoving his way through the crowd, he stooped to lift Winter into his arms, squeezing her against him. "I didn't know where you were . . . I didn't know . . ."

"What's happened?" said Levana, trying to push her way into the nursery.

"No, don't look. Don't go in there. It's horrible."

"I want to see, Papa."

"No, you don't, darling. No, you don't. Sweetheart—"

Levana bristled. Never did he call her that when they were in public, always hiding their relationship behind closed doors for fear of impropriety. He must have been truly shaken. He tried to grab her wrist, but she ripped her hand away. She had to see. She had to know.

"Move aside! She is my niece. Let me see her!"

The people listened. How could they not? Their faces

drawn in horror, cloths pressed over their mouths to stifle the stench of smoke and coals and . . . she thought, certainly that wasn't the smell of burning flesh? But it did have a familiar meatiness that turned her stomach.

When finally she reached the front of the crowd, she paused, taking in the sight through a veil of smoke. Dr. Eliot was there, along with countless guards, some still holding empty buckets that must have been used to put out the flames, others stamping out the remaining embers. The blanket was entirely gone, the playhouse reduced to a teetering wood structure, all blackened timbers and ashes. Scorch marks were left on the wallpaper and elaborate crown moldings.

Through the clustered guards, Levana could make out two bodies on the playhouse's upper level. Obviously bodies, though from this distance they looked like little more than charred remains.

"Step back! Step away!" Dr. Eliot screamed. "Give me room to look at her. Give me space. You're not helping!"

"Come away," Evret said, behind her again.

Shivering, Levana stepped back, and dared to turn to face him. She didn't have to fake the shock. The sight of it was a thousand times more terrifying than her imagination had given her. A thousand times more real.

She had done this.

Those bodies were her fault.

Selene was dead.

Though Evret was still holding Winter against his hip, and trying to block her view with his hands, Levana could see the girl craning her head to see the commotion and the chaos, the burned remains of her playhouse and her only cousin.

"Come away," Evret said again. He took Levana's hand, and she allowed him to guide her. Her thoughts were a daze as they made their way back through the corridors. Her stomach was writhing with a hundred emotions she couldn't have named. Winter's questions started coming in force. *What happened, Papa? Where is Selene? What's going on? Why does it smell like that?*

She went largely ignored, answered only by kisses pressed against her thick curls.

"She is dead," Levana murmured.

"It's horrible," said Evret. "A horrible, horrible accident."

"Yes. A horrible accident." Levana's grip tightened around his hand. "And now . . . you understand? This means I will be the queen."

Evret glanced at her, his face full of sorrow as he scooped his free arm around her shoulder and pulled her against him. He pressed a kiss against the top of her head then too.

"You don't need to think about that now, sweetheart."

But he was wrong.

As the knots in her stomach slowly began to loosen, it was all she could think of.

She was the queen.

The guilt and the horror and the memory of that awful smell might stay with her forever, but she was the queen.

PRINCESS SELENE WAS PRONOUNCED DEAD THAT EVENING. Levana made the announcement to the people from the palace's broadcast center. The video showed pictures of the young princess while Levana struggled to keep her voice somber, even while her nerves tingled from success. It was not happiness—she was very sad to know that victory had required such an appalling act. But success was success, victory was victory. She had done it and now, as the country mourned, she would be the one to lift them out of this tragedy.

Little Selene, barely three years old, would hardly even make a blip in their history. The memory of their little princess would be entirely eclipsed with the reign of Queen Levana.

The fairest queen that Luna had ever known.

For once, she was satisfied. She had Evret. She had her crown.

She did not yet have an heir, but now that she was the last of the royal bloodline, surely fate would smile on even this request. She was all that was left. Not having a child of her own was not an option. After all, Winter couldn't grow up to be queen. No. Levana would have a child.

With Selene gone, these were the new thoughts that engulfed her. How she would be a great ruler and how the people would love her with all their hearts. And how, when Levana finally gave Evret a child of their own, he too would love her, finally, even more than his darling Solstice.

She was making the life she'd always wanted for herself, and she was close to it now. So very, very close.

But only a week had gone by when Levana began to notice the change.

The way people dropped their eyes when she walked past, not with normal respect, but something akin to fear. Perhaps—was she imagining it? Perhaps even disgust.

The way there was a new coldness from the palace servants. How they all seemed to be biting their tongues, wanting to say something to her and daring not to.

The way that Evret asked her one night why she had gone to get Winter that day. Why she had brought it on herself to take Winter to the doctor's appointment when clearly it was something the nanny was capable of.

"What do you mean?" Levana asked, her heart in her throat. "She's my daughter, and I hardly get to spend time with her these days. Why shouldn't I take her to her appointments?"

"It's just . . ."

She tensed. "It's just *what*?"

"Nothing. It's nothing. I don't know what I was thinking."

He kissed her, and that was the last that was said of it.

But all this she could have ignored. Let them think she was guilty. Let them accuse her behind closed doors. As the queen of Luna and the only royal descendant of the Blackburn bloodline, no one would dare accuse her to her face.

No—it was another rumor that chilled Levana to her core.

They were saying that Selene had survived.

It was not possible.

It could not be possible.

She had seen the body, smelled the charred flesh, witnessed the aftermath of the fire. A tiny toddler could not have lived through that.

She was dead. She was gone.

It was over.

So why did she go on haunting Levana this way?

"I HOPE YOU KNOW THAT YOU ARE NOT IN ANY TROUBLE," said Levana. "I only want to make sure I know the complete truth."

Dr. Eliot stood before her in the center of the throne room. Normally this was the type of proceeding that would be dealt with in front of the entire court, but without knowing what, exactly, the doctor knew, Levana trusted very few people to listen to her testimony. She had even left her personal guards to wait in the corridor, for the last person she wanted to receive an account of this meeting was Evret, and even highly trained guards were not impervious to spreading gossip.

So it was only her, seated on her throne, and her trusted head thaumaturge, Sybil Mira, standing to the side with her hands tucked into the sleeves of her stark white coat.

"I have told you everything that I know, My Queen," said Dr. Eliot.

"Yes, but . . . there are rumors. I'm sure you've heard them. Rumors that say Princess Selene may have survived the fire? That *you*, as the first person to inspect the bodies, might have some information about what was found in the fire that you've chosen to keep hidden."

"I would hide nothing from you, My Queen."

She inhaled a patient breath. "She was my niece, doctor. I deserve to know the truth. If she is still alive, it would ... it would pain me very much to think that anyone would withhold that information from me. You know that I loved her as if she were my own."

Dr. Eliot pressed her lips, the look brief yet intense. "I am sure," she said, enunciating carefully, "that it would mean a *great* deal to you had the princess survived, My Queen. But when I saw the body after the fire, I'm afraid she was already lost. There was no saving her."

"No *saving* her." Levana leaned forward. "So you're saying that she wasn't dead yet?"

The doctor hesitated. "There was a faint heartbeat. This was mentioned in my report, Your Majesty. But while there was still some life in her when I arrived, she died shortly thereafter. I was there myself when the heartbeat stopped. She is dead."

Levana gripped the arm of her throne. "And where was that? When her heartbeat stopped. Was that still in the nursery?"

"Yes, My Queen."

"And was there anyone else there to witness it? Anyone who could vouch for your story?"

Dr. Eliot opened her mouth to speak, but hesitated. "I . . . yes, My Queen. By that time, Dr. Logan Tanner had arrived as well, having rushed over from the med-center."

Levana lifted an eyebrow. "Dr. Logan Tanner? I have not spoken to him."

"All due respect, My Queen, I'm sure you have more pressing matters than conducting your own investigation into this tragic incident. Dr. Tanner will not give you any more information than I already have. As you said, I was the first to see the princess's body. I can tell you with absolute certainty that she is dead."

Staring at the doctor, Levana could feel the woman's smugness rolling off her. She seemed anxious, but also confident.

She knew more than she was saying, and the knowledge of this itched beneath Levana's skin.

"All due respect," Levana said, feeling the words slithering in her mouth, "there is no more pressing matter than if my niece—our *future queen*—is alive. If this is true, and you choose to keep this information from me, you understand that it would be a high offense. It could be cause enough to have you tried as a traitor to the crown."

The doctor's smugness faded. She dipped her head. "I am sorry if I've caused any offense, My Queen. I did not mean to negate your concern over these rumors. It's only that I can tell you nothing more than I already have. I certainly wish that there was substance to these rumors, that our dear princess had survived the fire. But I'm afraid it simply isn't true."

Levana leaned back into her throne, her fingers gripping the thick, carved arms. Finally, she nodded. "I believe you, and I apologize for this added inconvenience, Dr. Eliot. You have certainly been a loyal subject for many years, and that has not gone unnoticed."

Dr. Eliot bowed. "Thank you, My Queen."

Levana dismissed the doctor and waited until the massive doors had shut behind her before speaking again. "Do you think she is lying, Sybil?"

"I'm afraid I do, My Queen. There is something in her air that I find distrustful."

"I agree. What can we do about it?"

Sybil came to stand in front of the throne. "It is essential that we uncover the truth of the aftermath of the fire. If Her Highness is alive, it is your right to know, as both our queen and the child's only relative. Otherwise, how else can you possibly seek to protect her from further harm?" Sybil's gray eyes glinted when she said *protect*, and Levana suspected that her head thaumaturge might know exactly why Levana was so set on finding out whether or not Selene was alive, but she also didn't think Sybil was too bothered by the truth. After all, Levana was the one who had raised her to her current position, bypassing several candidates with more experience. Some days she wondered if Sybil was the only person in her entourage who was truly loyal to her.

"Dr. Eliot seems to be under the impression that my interest in Selene's welfare is not born out of loving concern. How can I know that she is telling us everything when she seems set on keeping something hidden?"

Sybil smiled. "We thaumaturges are trained with certain methods of extracting information, even from those unwilling to give it. Perhaps Dr. Eliot and I should have a more private conversation."

Levana stared at her, wondering if she wanted to know what these extraction techniques might consist of, but almost as quickly recognizing that she would go to any lengths to find out the truth of her niece and what had happened in the nursery that day.

Besides, Sybil herself didn't seem opposed.

"Yes," she said, sitting taller. "I think that is a necessary course of action, Sybil. Though I fear other people on staff won't be as understanding."

"We will make them understand. After all, it is rather peculiar that Dr. Eliot was the first trained doctor to reach the child, and yet she wasn't able to rescue the girl, even after finding a heartbeat? The grounds for suspicion are obvious. It only makes sense that we would further investigate this matter."

Feeling her anxiety start to ease, Levana nodded. "You are entirely correct." She dug her fingernail into the carved ornamentation of the throne. "And once we have learned all we can from Dr. Eliot, I think it will benefit us to talk to this Logan Tanner as well. I want to know everything about the results of that fire."

Sybil bowed. "I will see that it is done, My Queen."

Dr. Eliot was taken into custody the next day for further questioning. Levana waited for Sybil's reports, having no interest in the details, but day after day passed in which the doctor told them nothing of value.

Then, two weeks later, before Levana could find a way to question the second doctor, this Logan Tanner, without raising further suspicion . . . he disappeared.

LEVANA REFUSED TO BE HAUNTED BY THE GHOSTS OF DEAD children and sisters, princesses and queens. In the year following Selene's death, she leaped into her role as the new, true queen of Luna.

She continued to strengthen the army, allocating as many resources as she could to allow the scientists to perfect the bioengineering processes. The first group of soldiers began their training, and they were even more miraculous than Levana had imagined. Half man, half beast, all brutality and viciousness. Levana made it her duty to become well acquainted with the surgeries and training of the soldiers. It was a beautiful sight, when the first boys emerged from their suspended-animation tanks, still dazed and awkward with their new instincts and mutated bodies.

And hungry. They awoke so very, very hungry.

She came to know the research team well, headed by the infamous Sage Darnel, though Levana was not as impressed with the old man as she'd expected to be after hearing of his genius for so many years. When she met him for the first time, she could think only of how this man had fathered a shell, and it took all her willpower to listen to his unenthusiastic explanations of the surgical procedures without making snide comments on his worthless offspring.

Meanwhile, the first carriers of the disease were sent to Earth. Levana had heard, years before during her parents' reign, that some of the citizens from the outer sectors would find ways to steal away in diplomatic or reconnaissance vessels heading to Earth, or pay what they could afford to persuade a supply pilot to whisk them away, leaving their life of labor behind. It was a selfishness that Levana couldn't fathom—to think that any of her people would consider only themselves and abandon the country that needed them.

Her parents had always turned a blind eye to these fugitives, perhaps not understanding that their society would crumble fast if they could not hold on to their limited labor supply.

But now Levana had a use for these runaways. As the strain of the disease was slipped into the outer sectors, each Lunar gradually became an unknown carrier, and their own immunity would mean they had no idea that they carried within their bodies a lethal disease.

It wasn't long before the first case of the disease was reported on Earth, in a tiny oasis town off the Sahara.

It spread quickly from there, raging through the Earthen Union like a wildfire. Though the Earthens hastened to set up quarantines for the sick, it was impossible to keep it contained when the secret carriers, the hapless Lunars, stayed so well disguised in their midst.

They called the disease *letumosis,* from an ancient language meaning death and annihilation, a fitting name as no one who caught the disease survived.

Levana and her court called it a success.

She didn't know how long it would take to weaken the

Earthens. Years, perhaps even decades, before the disease became the pandemic Levana envisioned. But she was already anticipating the time when she would swoop in and offer them an antidote. She was already dreaming of how the leaders of Earth would prostrate themselves before her. In their desperation, they would offer her anything. Any resource. Any land. Any alliance.

She would try to be patient, knowing that the day would come. She would try to ignore the pessimistic mutterings of her advisers and their reports that claimed all of the new labor initiatives she'd put into place were unsustainable. She would not back down now.

Everything was going according to plan. All that was required was patience.

Nearly fifteen months had passed since Selene's death when Levana was told that Dr. Sage Darnel, head of the bio-engineering team, had disappeared as well. Suicide, some suspected, although a body was never found. Many believed that he had never recovered from the birth and death of his shell daughter.

Yet another talented scientist, gone. But when Levana was informed that this would not halt the production of soldiers and that all surgeries would continue as scheduled, she forgot about the old man and his pathetic life entirely.

The years passed. Her legacy grew. The rumors of

Princess Selene began to fade. Finally, finally, Levana had everything she wanted.

Almost everything she wanted.

LEVANA STOOD ON THE PALACE LAWN, WATCHING AS EVRET chased Winter and Jacin around the lakeshore. She had finally relented to Evret's friendship with Garrison and his family, and now they were a permanent fixture in her life, despite how much she wished Evret would befriend some of the court families. The boy must have been eleven now, a couple years older than Winter, slender as a twig and still as pale as the white sand he trampled on. He and the princess, to Levana's dismay, seemed to have formed an inseparable attachment.

For her part, Princess Winter was growing up to be as beautiful as a love-sung lullaby. Her skin, a few shades lighter than Evret's, was velvet soft. Her hair had grown into thick curls, tight as springs and glossy as high-polished ebony wood. She had her mother's eyes, caramel, but with flecks of gray and emerald taken from her father.

Whispers were beginning to circulate. Whereas before, members of the court had mocked the idea of marrying a princess who was nothing more than a guard's child—now, moods were changing. Though still only a child, her beauty was becoming impossible to ignore. Such a child would no doubt grow up to be a stunning woman, and the families were taking notice.

Levana knew that this would benefit her someday. Her stepdaughter would be an ideal bargaining chip should the need for an alliance arise. And yet, the first time she overheard talk of how the princess might someday be even more fair to look on than the queen herself, Levana's thoughts had surged with hatred.

Levana had worked so hard to perfect her glamour. To be the most beautiful queen to ever sit on Luna's throne—more beautiful than her mother, more beautiful than Channary. No longer was she the ugly princess, the deformed child. The thought that Winter could so easily achieve what she had worked so hard for churned in Levana's stomach.

It did not help that Evret spoiled her mercilessly. They were never together for more than a moment before the dandy child was hoisted up on his shoulders or swung around like a spinning toy. Though Evret refused to ever dance with Levana at the royal balls, she had caught him teaching Winter what waltz steps he knew. His pockets seemed to always be full of those sour apple candies the princess was so fond of.

Levana reached for her throat, wrapping the Earth

pendant up in her fist. There had been a time when Evret brought *her* gifts too.

Down the shore, the children's laughter sparkled as bright as the sunlight on the lake's surface, and Evret laughed as much as any of them. Each note was a needle in Levana's heart, undoing her.

There had also been a time when Evret would have asked her to join them, but it was not queen-like to run and laugh and roll around in the sand. After she had waved away his requests too many times, he stopped making them, and now she regretted every time she'd stood by and watched.

Watched as Evret lifted a squealing Winter over his head.

Watched as Garrison's wife fixed them cheese sandwiches that were devoured as greedily as anything the royal chefs ever prepared.

Watched as Jacin showed Winter how to build a sandcastle and then how best to destroy it.

This was a family, all of them, happy and carefree.

And despite all her efforts, all her manipulations, Levana had never become a part of it.

"Sweetheart?"

She started, prying her attention away from the children to see Evret clomping toward her. His pants were soaked up to his knees and covered in white, sparkling sand.

He was as handsome as the first day she'd laid eyes on him, and she loved him every bit as much. Knowing that made her feel as hollow inside as carved-out wood.

"Is that the charm I gave you?" he asked, his teeth glinting in a refreshing smile. It melted her and stung at the same time.

Levana unclasped her hand. She hadn't realized that she was still gripping the old, tarnished charm.

"I didn't even know you still had it," said Evret. Reaching for her, he looped a finger beneath the chain. The touch was brief and deliberate and made her dizzy with the same spark of yearning she'd felt as a teenager.

"Of course I still have it. It was the first gift you gave me."

A shadow fell over his expression, one that she couldn't translate. Something sad and distant.

With a tap against her sternum, he let the charm go. "Are you just going to stand here watching all day?" he asked, eyes twinkling again. Maybe the shadow had been only her imagination.

"No," she said, unable to return more than a tired turn of her own lips. "I was about to go inside. There's a new trade contract with TX-7 I need to review."

"A trade contract? It can't wait until tomorrow?" He cupped her face in his hands. "You work too hard."

"A queen does not keep office hours, Evret. It is always a responsibility."

His expression turned scolding. "Even a queen has to relax sometime. Come on. Come play. It won't hurt you, and no one would *dare* to criticize if they saw."

He said it like a joke, but Levana thought for sure there was tension underlying it. "What does that mean?" she said, pulling away.

His hands fell to his sides.

"You think that people are afraid of me?" she pressed. "So *oppressed* that they wouldn't dare say something out of favor? Is that it?"

His jaw worked for a moment, baffled, before he set it in frustration. "People have always been afraid to speak out against the royal family—that's politics. It isn't something you alone can lay claim to."

Huffing, Levana turned on her heel and started marching back toward the palace.

With a groan, Evret chased after her. "Stop it. Levana. You're overreacting. I didn't mean anything by it."

"You must think I'm an awful ruler. One of those spoiled, selfish queens who cares more for her own reputation than the welfare of her people."

"That's not what I think. I know you care what the people

think about you, but I also know you care about them. In your own way."

"And what way is *that?*" she snapped, ducking into the palace's overhang.

"Levana, would you stop?"

His hand encircled her wrist, but she yanked it away. "Don't touch me!"

Immediately, the guards who were always in her periphery stepped forward, weapons at the ready.

Evret halted, raising his hands to show he meant no harm. But his expression was furious—and Levana knew that his honor was the reputation *he* cared to protect, that he would not be happy if anyone dared start a rumor that he had threatened the queen, his *wife,* when she was the one who was being absurd.

Overreacting.

"Fine," he said, taking a step back, before turning away entirely. "Go read your contract, Your Majesty."

Levana watched his retreating back, her hands clenched into shaking fists, before she marched toward the main stairs. It felt like running away. It felt like giving up.

When she reached her private solar, where she conducted most of her business, she sat down to review the trade contract, but immediately started to cry instead. She hadn't known the tears were coming until it was too late to stop them.

She cried for the girl who had never belonged. A girl who tried so hard, harder than anyone else, and still never had anything to show for it. A girl who had been certain that Evret loved her and only her, and now she couldn't even remember what that certainty felt like.

Despite every one of her weapons, the heart of Evret Hayle remained unconquered.

She wasn't even trying to get pregnant anymore, though she knew that couldn't last. It was only that for so long her visits to Evret's bedchambers had felt more exhaustive than passionate. More hopeless than anything.

She cried because she could feel the gossip rustling through the court, her barrenness a regular topic of closed-door conversations. Thaumaturges and family heads moved around the palace like pawns on a game board, forging alliances, plotting their moves should the throne ever be left without a suitable heir.

She cried because there would be bloodshed and uprisings should she fail. In the end, someone would place the crown on an undeserving head and a new royal bloodline would begin. Levana hadn't the faintest idea who would fall and who would rise to take her place.

She refused to give weight to those fears.

The throne needed an heir and *she* would be the one to produce it. The stars would smile on her eventually. They had to, for Luna's sake.

But fate would be on her side only if she could prove that she was the only ruler this country needed.

Luna *was* thriving. The city of Artemisia was more a paradise now than it had ever been. All of the outer sectors were producing goods at rates never before seen, and whenever there were rumors of unrest, Levana had only to complete a tour through the domes to visit her people and remind them that they were happy. That they loved her, and they would work for her without complaint. Being among her people was as close to a family as she'd yet to find.

The stronger Luna's economy grew, the more Levana wanted.

She cried now because she wanted so very, very much.

She wanted everything for her people.

She wanted Earth.

She *needed* Earth.

All of it. Every mountain. Every river. Every canyon and glacier and sandy shore. Every city and every farm. Every weak-minded Earthen.

Having control over the blue planet would solve all of her political problems. Luna's need for resources and land

and a larger labor force. She did not want to go down in history as the fairest queen this little moon had ever known. She wanted to be known through history as the fairest queen of the galaxy. As the ruler who united Luna and Earth under one monarchy.

The yearning grew quietly at first, taking the place in her belly where a child should have been. It thrived somewhere so deep inside her she hadn't even known it existed until one day she looked up at the planet hanging, mocking her, just out of reach, and she almost fell to her knees with the strength of her want.

The more time that passed, the more that desire dug its talons into her.

She deserved Earth.

Luna deserved Earth.

But despite all her plotting, all her long meetings spent discussing soldiers and plagues, she still wasn't sure how to take it.

"WHY IS IT ALWAYS A PRINCE?" ASKED WINTER. "WHY ISN'T she ever saved by a top-secret spy? Or a soldier? Or a . . . a poor farm boy, even?"

"I don't know. That's just how the story was written."

Evret brushed back a curl of Winter's hair. "If you don't like it, we'll make up a different story tomorrow night. You can have whoever you want rescue the princess."

"Like a doctor?"

"A doctor? Well—sure. Why not?"

"Jacin said he wants to grow up to be a doctor."

"Ah. Well, that's a very good job, one that saves more than just princesses."

"Maybe the princess can save herself."

"That sounds like a pretty good story too."

Levana peered through the barely open door, watching as Evret kissed his daughter's brow and pulled the blankets to her chin. She had caught the end of the bedtime story. The part where the prince and princess got married and lived happily for the rest of their days.

Part of her wanted to tell Winter that the story was a lie, but a larger part of her knew that she didn't much care what Winter did or didn't believe.

"Papa?" Winter asked, stalling Evret just as he moved to stand. "Was my mother a princess?"

Evret listed his head. "Yes, darling. And now she's a queen."

"No, I mean, my real mother."

Levana tensed, and she could see the surprise mirrored in Evret's posture. He slowly sank back down onto the bed's covers.

"No," he said quietly. "She was only a seamstress. You know that. She made your nursery blanket, remember?"

Winter's lips curved downward as she picked at the edge of her quilt. "I wish I had a picture of her."

Evret didn't respond. Levana wished that she could see his face.

When his silence stretched on for too long, Winter glanced up. She appeared more thoughtful than sad. "What did she look like?"

Like me, Levana thought. *Tell her. Tell her she looked like me.*

But then Evret shook his head. "I don't remember," he whispered. It was a sad confession, and it struck Levana between her ribs. She took a step back in the corridor. "Not exactly, at least," he amended at Winter's crestfallen expression. "The details have been stolen from me."

"What do you mean?"

His tone took on renewed buoyancy. "It isn't important. What I *do* remember is that she was the most beautiful woman on all of Luna. In the whole entire galaxy."

"More beautiful than the queen?"

Though she couldn't see his face, Levana could see the way that Evret flinched. But then he stood and leaned over his daughter, pressing another kiss into her full head of wild curls. "The most beautiful in the entire *universe,*" he said, "second only to *you.*"

Winter giggled, and Levana stepped away again, backing up until her back hit a solid wall. She tried to brush away the sting of rejection, the knowledge that she was still *not good enough*, not when compared with his precious Solstice and his lovely daughter. She pressed the feelings down, down, letting them turn hard and cold inside, while her face was smiling and pleasant.

When Evret emerged a moment later, he looked startled to find her there, but he covered it easily. He was not as good as some of the guards at disguising his emotions, but he had gotten better at it over the years.

"I wanted to tell you that I'm sorry," she said, "about this afternoon."

Shaking his head, Evret shut Winter's door, then headed down the hall to his own chambers.

Levana followed, wringing her hands. "Evret?"

"It doesn't matter." The lights flickered on as he entered the room and started taking off his boots. "Was there something you needed?"

Levana took in the bedroom she'd rarely seen in the light. Evret had never bothered to bring much personality into it. After ten years, the room still felt like a guest suite.

"I wanted to ask you why . . . why did you agree to marry me?"

He froze, briefly, before kicking the second boot across the room. "What do you mean?"

"In hindsight, I sometimes wonder. It seems that back then I had to coerce you for every kiss. Every moment we spent together you were fighting me. At the time I was so sure it was just you being...a gentleman. Honorable. Loyal to...Solstice's memory. But now I'm not so sure."

With a heavy sigh, Evret sank into a cushioned chair. "We don't have to talk about this now. What's done is done."

"But I want to know why. Why did you say yes, if you...if you didn't love me. And you didn't want to be royalty. And you didn't care if Winter was a princess. Why say yes?"

She could see him struggling through a long silence, before he shrugged. "I didn't have a choice."

"Of course you had a choice. If you didn't love me, you should have said no."

He laughed humorlessly, leaning his head against the chair's backrest. "No, I couldn't have. You made it very clear you weren't going to let me say no. Tell me I'm wrong. Tell me you would have just let me walk away."

Levana opened her mouth to say that, yes, of course, she would have allowed him his freedom, if that's what he'd truly wanted.

But the words didn't come.

She remembered that morning still so clearly. Her blood on the sheets. The taste of sour berries. The bittersweet memory of his caresses, knowing that he'd been hers for one night, and yet never hers at all.

No.

No, she would not have let him walk away.

She shuddered, her gaze dropping to the ground.

What a stupid child she'd been.

"At first I'd thought it was a game to you," Evret continued when it was clear he'd made his point. "Like it was with your sister. Trying to get me to want you like that. I thought you'd grow tired of me, and eventually you'd leave me alone." A line formed between his eyebrows. "But when you told me to marry you, I realized it was already too late. I didn't know what you would do if I fought you—*really* fought you. You're very good at your manipulations—you were even back then—and I knew I couldn't resist if you forced me to accept. And I worried that if I kept fighting, you might . . . you could do something rash."

"What did you think I was going to do?"

He shrugged. "I don't know, Levana. Have me arrested? Or executed?"

She laughed, although it wasn't funny. "Executed for what?"

His jaw tightened. "Think about it. You could have told

anyone that I'd forced myself on you, or threatened you, or—anything. You could have said anything, and it would be my word against yours, and we both know I would lose. I couldn't risk it. Not with Winter. I couldn't let you ruin what little I had left."

Levana stumbled backward as if she'd been struck. "I would never have done that to you."

"How was I supposed to know that?" He was practically yelling now, and she hated it. He almost never yelled. "You held all the power. You've *always* held all the power. It's so exhausting to fight you all the time. So I just went along with it. At least being your husband allowed Winter and me some protection. Not much, but . . ." He clenched his teeth, looking like he regretted telling her so much, and then shook his head. His tone quieted. "I figured that eventually you would tire of me, and I would take Winter far away from here, and it would be over."

Levana's heart throbbed. "It's been almost ten years."

"I know."

"And now? Are you still waiting for it to be over?"

His expression softened. The anger was gone, replaced with something infuriatingly kind, though his words were heartbreakingly cruel. "Are you still waiting for me to fall in love with you?"

She braced herself, and nodded. "Yes," she whispered.

His brow wrinkled. With sadness. With regret. "I'm sorry, Levana. I'm so sorry."

"No. Don't say that. I know that you lo—that you care about me. You're the *only* one who's ever cared about me. Ever since ... on my sixteenth birthday, you were the only one to give me a gift, remember?" She fished the pendant from beneath her collar. "I still wear it, all the time. Because of you. Because I love you, and I know ..." She gulped, trying in vain to swallow back her mounting sobs. "I know it means you love me too. You always have. *Please.*"

His eyes were wet too. Filled, not with love, but remorse.

In a broken voice, he said, "It was Sol's gift."

Levana froze. "What?"

"The pendant. It was Sol's idea."

The words trickled into her ears like a slow-draining faucet. "Sol ...? No. Garrison said it was from you. There was a card. It was from *you.*"

"She'd seen you admiring that quilt in her store," Evret said. His voice was tender, like speaking to a small child on the verge of a breakdown. "The one of Earth. That's why she thought you might like the pendant too."

She clutched the pendant in her fist, but no matter how tight she squeezed, she could feel her hope passing like water through her fingers. "But ... Sol? Why? Why would she ...?"

"I told her about how I'd seen you impersonating her. That day, before the coronation."

Levana's mouth went dry, the mortification she'd felt that day quick to return.

"I think she felt bad for you. She thought you must be lonely, that you needed a friend. So she asked me to look out for you, when I was at the palace." He gulped. "To be kind."

He seemed sympathetic, but Levana knew it was just a cover for his true feelings. Pity. He pitied her.

Sol had pitied her.

Sickly, irrelevant Solstice Hayle.

"The pendant was her idea," Evret said, looking away. "But the card was mine. I *did* want to be your friend. I did care about you. I still do."

She released the pendant faster than she would have released a burning ember.

"I don't understand. I don't—" She choked on a sob. She felt like she was drowning, and desperation was clawing at her, her lungs trying to breathe, but there was no air left. "Why can't you even *try*, Evret? Why can't you even try to love me?" Crossing the room, she knelt before him, taking his hands into hers. "If you would just let me love you, let me show you that I could be the wife you wanted, that we could—"

"Stop. Please, stop."

She gulped.

"You're always so desperate to make this work, to turn our marriage into something it isn't. Haven't you ever just stopped to wonder what else might be out there? What you might be missing out on by trying so hard to force this to be real between us?" He squeezed her hands. "I told you a long time ago that by choosing me, you were giving up your chance to find happiness."

"You're wrong. I can't be happy—not without you."

His shoulders sank. "Levana . . ."

"I mean it. Think about it. We'll start over. From the beginning. Pretend that I'm just a princess again, and you're the new royal guard, coming to protect me. We'll act like this is our first meeting." Suddenly giddy with the prospect, Levana leaped back to her feet. "You should start by bowing to me, of course. And introducing yourself."

He massaged his brow. "I can't."

"Of course you can. It can't hurt to try, not after everything we've been through."

"No, I can't pretend that we've never met, when you're still . . ." He flicked his fingers at her.

"Still what?"

"Still looking like *her.*"

Levana pursed her lips. "But . . . but this is how I look now. This is me."

Dragging his hand over his coiled hair, Evret stood. For a

moment, Levana thought he was going to play along. That he would bow to her, and they would begin anew. But instead, he shuffled around her and turned down the blankets on the bed. "I'm tired, Levana. Let's talk about this more tomorrow, all right?"

Tomorrow.

Because they would still be married tomorrow. And the day after that. And the day after that. For all eternity, he would be the husband who had never loved her. Wanted her. Trusted her.

She shuddered, more afraid than she'd been in a long, long time.

After so many years of wrapping herself in the glamour, it was nearly impossible to let it go. Her brain struggled to release her grip on the manipulation.

Heart hammering, she slowly turned around.

Evret was in the middle of pulling his shirt over his head. He tossed it on the bed and looked up.

Gasping, he stumbled back a step, nearly knocking a glowing sconce off the wall.

Levana shrank away, wrapping her arms around her waist. She ducked her head, so that her hair fell over half her face, hiding what it could. But she resisted the urge to cover her scars with her hands. She refused to pull up the glamour again.

The glamour he had always loved.

The glamour he had always hated.

At first, it seemed that he wasn't even breathing. He just stared at her, speechless and horrified. Finally, he closed his mouth and placed a shaking hand on the bedpost to steady himself. Forced down a gulp.

"This is it," she said, as new tears started to leak from her good eye. "The truth that I didn't want you to see. Are you happy now?"

His blinks were intense, and she could imagine how difficult it was for him to hold her gaze. To not look away, when he so clearly wanted to.

"No," he said, his voice rough. "Not happy."

"And if you had known this from the beginning, could you ever have loved me?"

His mouth worked for a long time, before he responded, "I don't know. I . . ." He shut his eyes, collecting himself, before meeting her full on. This time, he didn't flinch. "It's not the way you look, or don't look, Levana. It's that you have controlled and manipulated me for *ten years.*" His expression twisted. "I wish you would have shown me a long time ago. Maybe things would have been different. I don't know. But now we'll never find out."

He turned away. Levana stared at his back, feeling not

like a queen at all. She was a stupid child, a pathetic girl, a fragile, destroyed thing.

"I love you," she whispered. "That much has always been real."

He tensed, but if he had any response, she left before she could hear it.

"COME HERE, BABY SISTER. I WANT TO SHOW YOU SOMETHING." Channary smiled her warmest smile, waving Levana over excitedly.

Instincts told her to be cautious, as Channary's enthusiasm had turned into cruelty before. But she was hard to resist, and even as Levana's instincts were telling her to back away, her legs carried her forward.

Channary knew better than to use her gift on soft-minded children, especially her young sister. She'd been scolded by their nannies a hundred times.

In response, she'd only gotten more secretive about it.

Channary was kneeling before the holographic fireplace of their shared nursery, the gentle warmth in contrast to the roaring flames and crackling logs in the illusion. With the exception of celebratory candles, fire was strictly forbidden on Luna. The smoke would too quickly fill up the domes, poisoning their precious air supply. But holographic fireplaces had been popular for some time now, and Levana always liked to watch how the flames danced and defied predictability, how the wooden logs smoldered and crumbled and sparked. She would watch them for hours, amazed at how the fire seemed to always be burning low, eating into the logs, and yet never went out altogether.

"Watch," said Channary, once Levana settled beside her. She had set a small bowl of glittering white sand on the carpet, and now she took a pinch of the sand and flicked it at the holographic flames.

Nothing happened.

Gut tightening with apprehension, Levana looked at her sister. Channary's dark eyes were dancing with the firelight.

"They're not real, right?" Leaning over, Channary passed her hand through the flames. Her fingers came away unblemished. "Just an illusion. Just like a glamour."

Levana was still too young to have much control over her own glamour, but she did have a sense that it wasn't exactly the same thing as this holographic fireplace.

"Go ahead," said Channary. "Touch it."

"I don't want to."

Channary glared at her. "Don't be a baby. It isn't real, Levana."

"I know, but . . . I don't want to." Some instinct made Levana curl her hands in her lap. She knew it wasn't real. She knew the holograph wouldn't hurt. But she also knew that fire was dangerous, and illusions were dangerous, and being tricked into believing things that weren't real was often the most dangerous thing of all.

Snarling, Channary grabbed Levana's arm and tugged her forward, nearly pulling Levana's entire torso into the flames. Levana shrieked and struggled to pull back, but Channary held firm, holding her small hand into the glowing flames of the holograph.

She felt nothing, of course. Just that same subtle warmth that the fire always released, to make it seem more authentic.

After a moment, Levana's heartbeat started to temper itself.

"See?" said Channary, though Levana wasn't sure what point she'd just made. She *still* didn't want to touch the holograph, and as soon as her sister released her, she pulled her hand back and inched away on the carpet.

Channary ignored the retreat.

"Now—watch." Reaching behind her, Channary produced a book of matches that she must have taken from the altar in the great hall. She had struck one before Levana could begin to question it, and leaned over, pressing the match into the bottom of the holograph.

There should not have been anything flammable. The hearth should not have caught fire. But it wasn't long before Levana could see a new brightness among the smoldering logs. The real flame licked and sputtered, and after a while Levana could make out the edges of dried leaves charring and curling. The kindling had been hidden by the holograph before, but as the real fire took hold, its brightness far outshone the illusion.

Levana's shoulders knotted. A warning in her head told her to get up and walk away, to go tell someone that Channary was breaking the rules, to leave fast before the fire grew any larger.

But she didn't. Channary would only call her a baby again, and if Levana dared to get the crown princess in trouble, Channary would find ways to punish her later.

She stayed rooted to the carpet, watching the flames grow and grow.

Once they were almost as big as the holograph, Channary again reached into the little bowl of sand—or maybe it was sugar?—and tossed a pinch into the flames.

This time they turned blue, crackled and sparked and faded away.

Levana gasped.

Channary did it a few more times, growing more daring as her experiment succeeded. Two pinches at a time, now. Here, an entire handful, like little fireworks.

"Do you want to try?"

Levana nodded. Pinched the tiny crystals and tossed them into the flames. She laughed as the blue sparklers billowed up toward the top of the enclosure and crashed into the stone wall where there should have been a chimney.

Rising to her feet, Channary began searching through the nursery, finding anything that might be entertaining to watch burn. A stuffed giraffe that smoked and charred and took a long time to catch flame. An old doll shoe that melted and furled. Wooden game pieces that were slowly scorched beneath their protective glaze.

But while Levana was entranced by the flames—so very real, with their smell of ashes and the almost painful heat blasting against her face and the smoke that was darkening the wallpaper overhead—she could tell that Channary was growing more anxious with each experiment. Nothing was as enchanting as the simple, elegant blue and orange sparks from the sugar bowl.

Snip.

Jerking away, Levana turned just in time to see Channary toss a lock of brown hair into the flames. As the lock curled like springs, blackened, and dissolved, Channary giggled.

Levana reached for the back of her head, found the chunk that Channary had cut nearly to her scalp. Tears sprung into her eyes.

She made to scramble to her feet, but Channary was fast, grabbing her skirt in big handfuls. With a pull, Channary yanked Levana back onto the floor. She screamed and crashed to her knees, barely catching herself before her face could hit the floor too.

Even as Levana tried to roll away, Channary was catching the hem of Levana's dress between the scissor blades, and the sound of ripping fabric tore at Levana's eardrums.

"Stop it!" she screamed. When Channary kept a firm hold on her skirt and the tear escalated all the way to Levana's thighs, Levana locked her teeth, grabbed up as much of the fabric as she could, and yanked it out of Channary's grip.

A large shred of material was torn away and Channary cried out and fell backward into the fire. Shrieking, she quickly pulled herself out of the hearth, her face twisted in pain.

Levana gaped at her sister, horrified. "I'm sorry. I didn't mean to. Are you all right?"

It was clear that Channary was not all right. Her lips

were snarling, her gaze darkened with a fury Levana had never seen—and she had seen her sister's anger many, many times. She shrank back, her fists still gripping her skirt.

"I'm sorry," she stammered again.

Ignoring her, Channary reached a trembling hand for the back of her shoulder, and turned so that Levana could see her back. It had happened so quickly. The top part of her dress was charred, but nothing had caught fire. What Levana could see of her sister's neck was bright red and there were already small blisters forming above the dress's neckline.

"I'll call for the doctor," said Levana, climbing to her feet. "You should get water . . . or ice, or . . ."

"I was trying to save you."

Levana paused. Tears of pain were glistening in her sister's eyes, but they were overshadowed by the crazed look, glowing with fury. "What?"

"Remember, baby sister? Remember how I came in here and found you playing with a real fire in the fireplace? Remember how you fell in, thinking it wouldn't hurt you, just like the holograph? Remember how I got burned while trying to rescue you?"

Blinking, Levana tried to take a step back, but her feet were rooted to the carpet. Not from fear or uncertainty—Channary was controlling her limbs now. She was too young, too weak to get away.

Horror crept down her spine, covering her skin in goose-flesh.

"S-sister," she stammered. "We should put ice on your burns. Before ... before they get any worse."

But Channary's expression was changing again. The fury was contorting into something cruel and sadistic, hungry and curious.

"Come here, baby sister," she whispered, and despite the terror twisting inside Levana's stomach, her feet obeyed. "I want to show you something."

LEVANA COULDN'T STOP CRYING, NO MATTER HOW HARD she tried. The sobs were merciless and painful, coming so fast she felt faint from an inability to breathe as her lungs convulsed. She crumpled over her knees, rocking and trembling. She wanted to stop crying. So badly she wanted to stop crying, in no small part because she knew that Evret, in his own private chambers down the hall, could probably hear her. And at first she'd dreamed that he would take pity on her, that the sound of her tears would soften his heart and bring him to her side. That he would comfort her and hold her and finally, *finally* realize that he'd loved her all along.

But she'd been crying long enough now, with no sign of

her husband, to know that it wasn't going to happen. Just one more fantasy that wouldn't come true. Just one more lie she'd constructed for herself to escape into, never realizing she was welding the bars of her own cage.

Finally, the tears began to slow, the pain began to dull.

When she could breathe again, and thought she could stand without collapsing, she took hold of a bedpost and hauled herself to her feet. Her legs were weak, but they held. Without the strength to reinstate her glamour, she tore off one of the sheer drapes that hung from the bed's canopy and draped it over her head. She would look like a ghost wandering the palace halls, but that was fine. She felt like a ghost. No more than a figment of a girl.

Hugging the makeshift veil around her body, she stumbled out of her bedroom. Two guards were posted outside the royal chambers, at silent attention as she emerged. If they were surprised at the fabric draped over her head, their expressions gave nothing away, and they fell into a march at a respectful distance behind her.

Despite the care she took to conceal herself, she passed no one else as she wandered through the palace. Even the servants were asleep this late at night.

She didn't know where she was going until, minutes later, she found herself standing outside her sister's bedroom, or what had been her sister's bedroom during her short reign as queen, nearly eight years ago. Levana could have taken these chambers as her own—larger and more lavish than the room she was currently in—but at the time she'd enjoyed the quaintness of her rooms shared with Evret and Winter. She'd liked the idea that she was a queen who did not need riches and luxuries, only the love of her family to surround her.

She wondered if the people of the court had been laughing behind her back all this time. Was she the only one who had never recognized just how false her marriage, her *family*, really was?

Leaving the guards in the hall, she opened her sister's door. It wasn't locked, and at first Levana expected to find it emptied of anything of value. Surely the servants knew that she never came here, that they could have their pick of all the fine treasures inside.

But as Levana stepped into the room and the lights flickered on, casting the room in a serene glow, it was exactly as she remembered it, even the very faint scent of her sister's perfume. It was like walking into a museum, every piece encapsulated in time. Her sister's hairbrush on the vanity, though the tines had been carefully picked clean. The unruffled bedcovers. There was even the little basinet with its cream-colored velvets and filigree of a tiny coronet on top, where baby Selene had slept, unbeknownst even to Levana.

She'd assumed that the child stayed with a wet nurse or nanny during that first year, not in her mother's own chambers.

It occurred to her, staring at that tiny, beautiful little bed, sweet and innocent and harmless, that she probably should have felt something. Remorse. Guilt. Horror at what she'd done all those years ago.

But there was nothing. She felt nothing but the breaking of her own heart inside her chest.

Tearing her gaze away, she spotted what she'd come for. Her sister's mirror.

It stood in the far corner, its glass cast in shadows. It was taller than Levana, framed in silver that was tarnished with age. The metal had been crafted into elaborate scrolls with a prominent crown centered at the top. On the sides, silver flowers and thorny branches entwined around the frame, looking as though they were growing out from behind the mirror, like they would someday engulf it entirely.

Levana had stood before a mirror only once since she was six years old. Since Channary had forced her into that fireplace—first her hand, then her arm, then the entire left side of her face. Offering no mercy. Channary didn't even have to touch her. Under the grip of Channary's mind control, Levana had been powerless to fight back, to run away, to pull herself from the flames.

Only when her screaming had brought a couple of servants running into the nursery did Channary let her go and told them all that she'd been trying to help her sister. Her stupid, curious baby sister.

Her ugly, deformed, scarred baby sister.

The mirror had belonged to their mother, and Levana had only faint memories of watching Queen Jannali primp in front of it before some gala or another, on those rare occasions when she wasn't annoyed with the presence of her own offspring. For the most part Levana remembered her mother as her glamour had been. Pale as a corpse with platinum hair and those severe violet eyes that seemed to make the rest of her fade away. But when she sat in front of this mirror, Jannali had been as she was underneath. As she was *really*. And she looked a lot like Channary, with naturally tanned skin and shiny brown hair. She'd been pretty. Perhaps even prettier than she was with the glamour—though not as striking. Not as regal.

Levana could recall being very, very young and having nightmares about her mother and the court and how everyone around her had two faces.

Channary claimed the mirror almost immediately following the assassinations, and Levana hadn't seen it since. Which was fine with her. She hated mirrors. Hated their reflections, their *truths*. Hated how she seemed to be the only one who hated them as much as she did, even when everyone in the entire court walked around with glamours every bit as fake as her own.

Now Levana braced herself and strolled toward the standing monstrosity. Her reflection came into view, draped with the sheer white cloth, and she was surprised to find that she didn't look so much like a ghost. Rather, she looked like a second-era bride. Endless happiness could be concealed beneath this veil. Boundless joy. So many dreams fulfilled.

Gripping the edges of the drape, she lifted it over her head.

She grimaced, flinching away from her reflection. It took her a moment to gather her courage again before she could face it, and even then she kept her face partly turned away, so that she could quickly turn back if the sight became too painful.

It was worse than she'd remembered, but then, she'd spent many, many years refusing to remember.

Her left eye was permanently sealed shut, and the scarred tissue on that side of her face was formed of ridges and grooves. Half of her face was paralyzed from the incident, and great chunks of hair would never grow back. The scars continued down her neck and shoulder, half of her chest and upper ribs, all the way down to her hand.

The doctors had done what they could at the time. They saved her life, at least. They told her that, when she was older, she would have options. A series of skin-grafting surgeries could gradually replace the ruined flesh. Hair transplants. Modified bone structure. They had even said that they could find a new, working eye for her. Finding a perfect match would be difficult but they would scour the entire country for a suitable donor, and surely, no one would dare refuse a request from their princess should she ask. Even their own eye.

But there would always be scars, no matter how faint, and at the time, the idea of accepting such transplants had disgusted her. Someone else's eye. Someone else's hair. Skin transplanted from the back of her thigh onto her own face. At the time, it had seemed easier to develop her glamour and pretend that nothing was wrong underneath it at all.

By now, so many had forgotten what she truly looked like she wouldn't even consider having the surgeries. She couldn't stand to think of those surgeons hovering over her unconscious, grotesque body, analyzing the best way to disguise her hideousness.

No. Her glamour worked. Her glamour *was* the reality now, no matter what Evret thought. No matter what anyone thought.

She was the fairest queen Luna had ever known.

Grabbing for the sheer drape, she pulled the veil back over her head, encapsulating herself. Her heart was stampeding now, her pulse drumming against her ears.

With an enraged scream, she reached for the silver hairbrush on the vanity and hurled it as hard as she could at the mirror.

A spiderweb of cracks burst across the glass, spindling toward the silver frame. A hundred veiled strangers looked back at her. She screamed again and grabbed for anything in reach—a vase, a perfume bottle, a jewelry box—throwing them all at the mirror, watching as pieces of glass splintered and shattered, broken slivers crashing to the floor. Finally she picked up the small chair beside the vanity, cushioned in white velvet.

With that final crash, the mirror was destroyed, shards of glass scattering halfway across the bedroom.

The guards burst through the door. "Your Majesty! Is everything all right?"

Panting, Levana threw the chair aside and crumpled to her knees, ignoring the piece of glass that cut into her shin. Trembling, she adjusted the veil over her head, making sure she was fully hidden.

"Your Majesty?"

"Don't come any closer!" she yelled, holding out her hand.

The guards paused.

"I want—" Nearly choking on the words, she scrubbed the tears from her face. It was a struggle to compose herself, but her voice was firm when she spoke again. "I want all the mirrors in the palace destroyed. Every one of them. Check the servants' quarters, the washrooms, everywhere. Check the entire city! Destroy them and throw their shattered pieces into the lake where I will never have to look at them again!"

After a long silence, one of the guards murmured, "My Queen."

She could not tell if his words were to say that it would be done, or that she was talking like a madwoman.

She didn't care.

"Once all of the mirrors are destroyed, I want to commission special glass for the palace, to replace all of the windows, and every glass surface. Glass that holds no reflection. None at all."

"Is that possible, My Queen?"

Exhaling slowly, Levana grabbed for the edge of the vanity and pulled herself to her feet as gracefully as she could. She adjusted the veil again before turning to face the guards. "If it is not, then we will all live in a palace without any glass at all."

"YES. YES. THIS WILL WORK. I'M PLEASED."

The technician bowed, his face contorted with obvious relief, but Levana was already ignoring him, her attention captured by the special screen she'd commissioned to be installed into the silver frame of her sister's mirror. The destroyed glass had been thrown into the lake with all the rest of it.

She drew a finger across the screen, testing its functionality. Most of the entertainment on Luna was broadcast through the holograph nodes or on the enormous screens set into the walls of the domes themselves. But comms and video feeds from Earth didn't always translate to the holographs, so her newly commissioned netscreen was more akin to Earthen technology. It was as useful as it was beautiful. She would need it for the surveillance she hoped to conduct on the people of the outer sectors. For her discussions with the Commonwealth emperor. For the newsfeeds she would be monitoring, closely, once her army was unleashed.

A good queen was a well-informed queen.

She paused when one of the Earthen newsfeeds showed the royal family of the Eastern Commonwealth. Emperor Rikan standing alone at the podium with his country's flag like a sunrise behind him. The young prince stood beside a sour-faced political adviser, his eyes downcast. He was a string bean of a child, not much older than Winter. But it was his father, expression equally miserable, that held Levana's attention.

The press conference was to discuss their recent tragedy.

The beloved empress was dead, having contracted none other than Levana's disease during a philanthropic trip to a plague-ridden town at the western edge of the Commonwealth.

Dead of letumosis.

Levana laughed—she couldn't help herself—remembering Channary's dreamy, offhanded comment that the empress might someday find herself assassinated.

This was not an assassination. This was not murder.

This was fate.

Simple, exquisite, blindingly obvious fate.

No longer could Earth flaunt its perfect royal family, in their perfect little palace, on their perfect little planet. No longer could they claim the happiness that had eluded Levana for so long.

"My Queen?"

She turned back to the technician. He was clutching a pair of gloves in his hands, and he looked terrified.

"Yes?"

"I only wanted to mention that...you are aware, I hope, that your—that glamours do not translate through netscreens? Should you wish to send any video comms, or conduct any broadcasts, that is."

A smile stretched across Levana's lips. "Do not worry. I have already commissioned something special from my dressmaker for just such an occasion." She glanced at the sheer lacy veil that had been delivered a few days before, much more sophisticated than the canopy curtains, yet with all the same mystery and security they'd afforded her.

Dismissing the technician, Levana turned back to watch the muted feed of the Commonwealth's royal family. Since her fight with Evret over a month before and her assault on the palace's mirrors, she'd delved into her role as queen more than she'd ever done before. She hardly slept. She hardly ate. She and Sybil Mira and the rest of the court spent long hours discussing trade and manufacturing agreements between the outer sectors, and new methods to increase productivity. More guards were needed to patrol the outer sectors—so more guards were drafted and began their training. Some of the young men they'd tried to draft didn't want to *be* guards at all, especially those who had family in the same sectors they would be monitoring. Levana solved the problem by threatening the livelihoods of those very families they were so concerned about, and watched how quickly the young men changed their minds. The curfew, instated for the necessary rest and protection of the workers, had not been popular to begin with, but after Levana had suggested they make public examples of those civilians who refused to obey the new laws, the people began to see the reasonableness of such strict expectations.

Even as she was making her country stronger and more stable, there was one burgeoning problem that Levana couldn't ignore.

Luna's resources were dwindling faster than ever, just as the reports had said they would. Only regolith seemed to be in endless supply, but their water and agriculture, their forest industry and metal-recycling plants were all dependent on the space within the atmosphere-and-gravity-controlled domes, and the materials that had been brought up from Earth so many generations ago.

More luxuries, more diverse crops, more military weaponry and training grounds and shipbuilding, all equaled fewer resources.

The court representatives warned her that they could not sustain this level of advancement for more than a decade or two.

On the screen, Emperor Rikan was leaving the stage. The crown prince was fidgeting with his necktie. The people of the Commonwealth were crying.

"Earth," Levana whispered, tasting the word on her tongue, and it felt like the first time she'd said it. Or, the first time she'd meant it. *Earth.* "That is what we need."

And why shouldn't they take it? They were the more advanced society, the more advanced species. They were stronger, and smarter, and more powerful. Earthens were but children in comparison.

But how best to take it? There were far too many Earthens to brainwash, even if she divided her entire court among them. Though letumosis was spreading—it would be years still before she could make use of her antidote. And her wolf soldiers were not yet ready for any sort of full-scale attack. There was still so much work to be done if she had any hope of taking Earth by force.

But as she learned from Channary, one did not always have to take things by force. Sometimes it was better if you made them come to you. Made them *want* you.

A marriage alliance then, just as Channary had dreamed for herself, all those years ago. Princess Winter would make a good match for this boy, but Winter had no royal blood. The alliance would be too superficial.

No, it had to be the queen. It had to be Levana. It had to be someone who could, someday, *someday*, produce an heir to the throne.

Pressing her lips, she turned off the screen.

She would have to do it, she knew. For the people. For their future. For Luna.

For all of Earth.

SHE COULD NOT REMEMBER THE LAST TIME SHE'D COME TO his chambers in the middle of the night, and Evret seemed surprised by her presence. They had barely spoken since their argument, and when Levana tried to kiss him, he rejected her as kindly as he could.

Still, he didn't ask her to leave.

She wondered if he was remembering her as she was beneath the glamour, and the thought hardened her heart. The way he had looked at her—the real her—iced her veins.

She stripped away his resistance, piece by piece. So gradually and gently he wouldn't even know she was tampering with him. He would think it was his own heart beating a little faster. His own blood running a little hotter. His own yearning growing inside him as he finally gave in and pulled her into his arms.

Love is a conquest.

Even knowing that it wasn't his choice, would never have been his choice, his kisses still elated her. Even after all these years, she loved him. No matter what he said about their marriage, that much was real.

Afterward, Levana stayed curled up in the crook of his arm, her head pressed against the hollow of his chest, listening to the lulling drum of his heartbeat. She ran her thumb over the stone wedding band he'd given her, twirling it around and around her finger. She knew that she would never again wear the Earth pendant after this night, but this band she would never take off. She would carry it with her for always, for eternity.

The pendant represented the love Evret had never had for her.

But the wedding band represented the love she had always had for him.

Love is a war.

Though she'd been expecting the muffled thumps from the corridor, she still startled when she heard them. Two royal guards, incapacitated. She wondered if he decided to kill them or merely knock them unconscious.

Evret stirred in his sleep. His arm tightened instinctively around her and Levana squeezed her eyes shut before she could cry.

From this day forward, you will be my sun at dawn and my stars at night.

The bedroom door burst open, crashing loud against the wall. Evret jolted upward, simultaneously pushing Levana aside.

A dark silhouette filled the door frame.

Later, when she had time to process it all, Levana would be amazed at how quickly Evret reacted. Even pulled from sleep, his instincts were immediate and alert. In one movement he shoved Levana off the bed so that she was protected behind the mattress and rolled himself off the other side. A gunshot flared through the room. The sound was deafening. It wouldn't be long before more guards came running.

"Majesty, stay down!" Evret yelled. From somewhere, he had a knife. Of course he had a knife. He had probably slept with it under his pillow since their wedding night and Levana had never known.

She didn't stay down. Instead, she gripped the tumbled blankets and watched as Evret flung himself toward the intruder, and she silently said her good-byes, even as tears trekked down her face.

The knife was only a hair from the intruder's chest when it froze.

This was not a shell like the one that killed her parents. This was a much more skilled assassin. A much more dangerous one. As Levana's vision adjusted to the light pouring in from the corridor, she watched Evret's eyes widen in recognition.

Although Head Thaumaturge Haddon had retired some years before, he had never fully left the court. Or, as Levana had guessed, fully given up on his ambitions. He had reached the highest position in court that he could achieve without being royalty himself.

Levana had made him a very tempting promise. He hadn't even hesitated when she told him her price.

The knife fell, landing anticlimactically on the bed.

A second gunshot. A third. A fourth. Blood splattered across the white linens. Down the hall, Levana heard Princess Winter screaming. She wondered whether the girl would come see what was happening or whether she would be smart enough to run for help.

Either way, it would be too late.

It was too late.

Joshua Haddon released Evret, who fell to his knees, blood covering his hands as he pressed them over his stomach. "Majesty—" he croaked. "*Run*."

The thaumaturge turned toward Levana. He was smiling, proud and haughty. He had succeeded. He had done as she had asked. And now, without the burden of a husband, it would be time for Levana to fulfill the promise she had made. To marry Joshua and crown him as the king of Luna. When

Levana asked him to do this, she was sure to tell him how she had admired him for so many years—that this is what she had longed for ever since she'd made the mistake of her youthful marriage. Arrogant as he was, Haddon took very little convincing.

Levana climbed onto her shaky legs.

Haddon lowered the gun. His eyes roved over her body—her glamour's body—full of lust and anticipation.

Ignoring the tears now drying on her cheeks, Levana flung herself toward Haddon. He lifted his arms to accept the embrace.

Instead, he received a knife, handle deep, in his chest.

As horror and comprehension crashed into his expression, Levana shoved him away. He stumbled back, collapsing against the wall.

She fell to the floor beside Evret. Agony clawed up her throat and exploded in a shrill wail.

As soon as Levana was out of danger, his last reserves of energy left him and Evret slumped against the side of the bed.

"Evret!" she cried, surprised to find that her terror was real. Watching the spark dim behind his eyes, the way those gray and emerald specks seemed to fade in the darkness, was more painful than she'd imagined it would be.

I vow to love and cherish you for all our days.

"Evret," she said again, whimpering now. Her hands joined his, trying to block the wounds. Down the hall there were new footsteps. It could not have been more than a minute since Haddon had entered the room, yet it felt like a lifetime had passed. Looking down, she saw blood splattered across her nightgown. Blood covering their hands. Blood on the two wedding bands he still wore, pressed up against each other.

Here is what I think of love.

She sobbed. "I'm sorry. I'm so sorry. Oh, stars. *Evret.*"

"It's all right," he gasped, dragging his arms around her and pulling her against him. "It's all right, sweetheart."

She cried harder.

"Please. Please. Take care of Winter."

She sobbed.

"Promise, My Queen. Promise you'll take care of her."

She dared to meet his eyes. They were intense and melting and struggling so hard to stay strong. To hide his pain. To pretend that he wasn't dying.

At some point, guards arrived. A doctor. Even Winter, with her pale nightgown and frightened tears. And Sybil, too, unsurprised it seemed, by the expressionless set of her brow.

Levana hardly saw any of them. She was alone with Evret, her husband, her beloved, clutching his hand as the blood cooled on her skin. She felt it the moment he was gone, and she was left alone.

She could not stop crying.

It was all her fault. Everything was her fault. She had ruined every moment she had with him, from their very first kiss.

"I promise," she whispered, though the words burned her throat. She did not love the child. She had only loved Evret, and now she had destroyed even that. "I promise."

Reaching for the pendant around her neck, she broke the chain with a firm yank. She slipped the charm into Evret's hand as Sybil pulled her away, and a screaming Winter collapsed against her father to take her place.

Her sister's words came back to her, thundering in her ears, filling up all the hollow places in her heart.

Love is a conquest. Love is a war.

Here is what I think of love.

Acknowledgments

Thank You, Thank You, Thank You . . .

To Jill, Cheryl, and Katelyn, for all your guidance and enthusiasm, and for not batting an eye when I was like, "Surprise! I wrote this thing, and I have no idea what to do with it."

To Liz, Jean, and Jon, for believing in me as an author, and for believing in Levana's story as one that needed to exist in the world.

To Rich Deas, for the most outstanding book covers a writer could ever hope for.

To the rest of the Macmillan team, for your tireless creativity and constant efforts on behalf of myself and the Lunar Chronicles.

To all of the folks behind NaNoWriMo, for reminding me every year what I'm capable of when I really put my mind to it.

To Tamara Felsinger, Jennifer Johnson, and Meghan Stone-Burgess, for being brilliant yet again.

To Jesse, for making me laugh even when the writing gets all depressing and stuff.

And lastly, to that girl who came to the *Cress* launch party dressed up as Queen Levana and pretended to kill me with her crazy-long fingernails. Thank you for not actually killing me with your crazy-long fingernails . . . Your Majesty.

Chapters 1-3 from

Winter

The final book of the
Lunar Chronicles

By Marissa Meyer

(coming in Fall 2015)

BOOK

One

She had a little daughter who was as white as snow,

as red as blood, and as black as ebony wood.

One

WINTER'S TOES HAD BECOME ICE CUBES. THEY WERE AS
cold as space. As cold as the dark side of Luna. As cold as—

"...security feeds captured him entering the AR-
Central med-clinic's sublevels at 2300 U.T.C...."

Thaumaturge Aimery Park smiled as he spoke, his voice
serene and measured, like a ballad. It was easy to lose track
of what he was saying, easy to let all the words blur and
conjoin. Winter curled her toes inside her thin-soled shoes,
afraid that if they got any colder before this trial was over,
they would snap off.

"...was attempting to interfere with one of the shells
currently stored..."

Snap off. One by one.

"...records indicate the shell child was the accused's
son, taken on 29 July of last year. He is now fourteen months
old."

Winter gripped her hands in her lap, hiding them in the folds of her gown. They were shaking again. It seemed like she was always shaking these days. She squeezed her fingers to hold them still. Pressed the bottoms of her feet into the hard floor. Struggled to bring the throne room into focus before it dissolved entirely.

The view was striking from the central tower of the palace. From here, Winter could see Artemisia Lake mirroring the white palace back up to the sky and the city that spread to the very edge of the enormous clear dome that sheltered them from the outside elements—or lack thereof. The throne room itself was built to extend past the walls of the tower, so that when one passed beyond the edge of the mosaic floor, they found themselves on a ledge of clear glass. Like standing on air, about to plummet into the depths of the crater lake.

To Winter's left, she could make out the edges of her stepmother's fingernails as they dug into the arm of her throne, an imposing seat carved from white stone. Normally, her stepmother was calm during these proceedings, and would listen patiently to the trials without a hint of emotion. Winter was used to seeing Levana's fingertips leisurely stroking the polished arm of her throne, not throttling it. But tension had been high in the palace since Levana and her entourage had returned from Earth, and her stepmother had flown into even more rages than usual these past months.

Ever since that runaway Lunar—that *cyborg*—had escaped from her Earthen prison.

Ever since war had begun between Earth and Luna.

Ever since the queen's betrothed had been kidnapped, and Levana's chance to be crowned empress had been stolen from her.

Winter tore her eyes away from the queen's fingers. The blue planet hung above them in an endless black sky, looking like someone had taken a knife to it and shorn it perfectly in half. They were a week into the long night, and the city of Artemisia was aglow with pale blue lampposts and glowing crystal windows, the lights dancing across the lake's surface and reflecting off the dome's ceiling.

One week. Yet Winter felt that it had been years since she had last seen the sun.

"How did he know about the shells?" Queen Levana asked, her voice echoing off the smooth surfaces of the throne room. "Why did he not believe his son to have been killed at birth?"

Seated around the rest of the room, in four tiered rows, were the families. The queen's court. The nobles of Luna, granted favor with Her Majesty for their generations of loyalty, their extraordinary talents with the Lunar gift, or pure luck at having been born a citizen of the great city of Artemisia.

Then, pitifully outnumbered, was the man on his knees beside Thaumaturge Park. He had not been born so lucky.

His hands were clasped together, pleading. Winter wished she could tell him that it wouldn't matter. All his begging would be for nothing. She felt there would be comfort in knowing there was nothing you could do to avoid death. Those who came before the queen having already accepted their fate seemed to have an easier time of it.

Tearing her gaze from the man, she stared at her own hands, still clawed around her gauzy white skirt. Her fingers too, she saw, had been bitten with frost. It was sort of pretty. Glistening and shimmering and *cold so very cold...*

"Your queen has asked you a question," said Aimery.

Winter flinched, as if he'd been yelling at her.

Focus. She must try to focus.

She lifted her head again and inhaled.

Aimery was wearing white now, having replaced Sybil Mira as the queen's head thaumaturge. The gold embroidery on his coat shimmered as he paced around the captive.

"I am sorry, Your Majesty," the man said, his voice restrained. Winter couldn't tell if he was disguising hatred for his sovereign, or merely trying to keep from turning into a blubbering mess. "My family and I have served you loyally for generations. I am a janitor at that med-clinic, and I'd heard rumors, you see. It was none of my business, so I never cared, I never listened. But . . . when my son was born a shell . . ." He whimpered. "He is my *son.*"

"Did you not think," said Levana, her voice loud and crisp, "that there might be a reason your queen has chosen to keep your son and all the other ungifted Lunars separate from our citizens? That we may have a purpose that serves the good of *all* our people by containing them as we have?"

The man gulped, hard enough that Winter could see his Adam's apple bobbing. "I know, My Queen. I know that you use their blood for some . . . experimentation. In your laboratories. But . . . but you have *so many,* and he's only a baby, and . . ."

"Not only is his blood valuable to the success of our war efforts and our political alliances, the likes of which I cannot expect a janitor from the outer sectors to understand, but he is also a shell, and his kind have proven themselves to be dangerous and untrustworthy, as you *will* recall from the assassinations made on King Marrok and Queen Jannali eighteen years ago. Yet you would subject our society to this threat?"

The man's eyes were wild with fear. "Threat, My Queen? He is a *baby.*" He paused. He did not look outright rebellious, but his lack of remorse would be sending Levana into a fury soon enough. "And the others that I saw in those tanks . . . so many of them, children. Innocent *children*."

The room seemed to chill.

Clearly, he knew too much. The shell infanticide had been in place since the rule of Levana's sister, Queen Channary, after a shell sneaked into the palace and killed their parents. Many citizens, but certainly not all, had been convinced that the precaution was necessary, and no one would be pleased to know that their babies had not been killed at all, but really locked away and used as tiny blood platelet manufacturing plants.

Winter blinked, imagining her own body as a blood platelet manufacturing plant.

Her gaze dropped again to her fingers, and she saw that the ice had extended nearly to her wrists now.

That would not be beneficial for the platelet conveyor belts.

"Does the accused have a family?" asked the queen.

Aimery bobbed his head. "Records indicate a daughter, age nine. We have not been able to locate her, but a search is underway. He has also two sisters, two nephews, and one niece. All live in Sector GM-12."

"No wife?"

"Dead five months past, of regolith poisoning."

The prisoner watched the queen, desperation pooling in his eyes.

The court began to stir, their vibrant clothes shifting and fluttering. This trial had gone on too long. They were growing bored.

Levana leaned against the back of her throne. "You are hereby found guilty of trespassing and attempted theft against the crown. This crime is punishable by immediate death."

The man shuddered, but his face remained pleading, hopeful. It always seemed to take them a few seconds to comprehend such a sentence.

"Your family members will each receive a dozen public lashings, to remind everyone in your sector that they cannot possibly comprehend the inner workings of our government and that I will not tolerate my decisions being questioned again."

The man's head started to droop, his jaw going slack.

"Your daughter, when she is found, will be given as a gift to one of the court's families. There, she will be taught the obedience and humility that one can assume she has not learned beneath your tutelage."

"No, please. Let her live with her aunts. She hasn't done anything!"

"Aimery, you may proceed."

"*Please!*"

"Your Queen has spoken," said Thaumaturge Aimery. Though he didn't raise his voice, it rumbled through the throne room into the ears of the lower-ranking thaumaturges, the guards, the court, the waiting servants, and the queen—the only judge and jury. His voice was suffocating. "Her word is final."

Aimery drew a knife from one of his bell-shaped sleeves and held the handle out to the prisoner, whose eyes had gone wide with hysteria.

The room grew colder. Winter noticed that her breaths were turning to fogged ice crystals. She shivered and squeezed her arms tight against her body.

The prisoner took the knife handle. His hand was steady. The rest of him was trembling.

"Please. My little girl—I'm all she has. *Please.* My Queen. Your Majesty!"

He raised the blade to his throat.

This was when Winter looked away. When she always looked away. She watched her own fingers burrow into her dress, her fingernails scraping at the fabric until she could feel the sting on her thighs. She watched the ice climb over her wrists, toward her elbows. Where the ice touched, her flesh went numb.

She imagined lashing out at the queen with those ice-solid fists. She imagined her hands shattering into a thousand icicle shards.

It was at her shoulders now. Her neck.

Even over the popping and cracking of the ice, she heard the cut of flesh. The burble of blood. A muffled gag. The hard slump of the body.

Bile squirmed up Winter's throat. The cold had stolen into her chest. She squeezed her eyes shut, reminding herself to be calm, to breathe. She could hear Jacin's steady voice in her head, his hands gripping her shoulders. *It isn't real, Princess. It's only an illusion.*

Usually it helped, even just the memory of him coaxing her through the panic. But this time, it seemed to prompt the ice on. Encompassing her rib cage. Gnawing into her stomach. Hardening over her heart. Freezing her from the inside out.

Listen to my voice.

Jacin wasn't there.

Stay with me.

Jacin was gone.

It's all in your head.

She heard the clomping of the guards' boots as they approached the body. The corpse being slid toward the ledge. The shove. Moments later, the splash down below.

The court applauded with quiet politeness.

Winter felt her toes snap off. One. By. One.

She was almost too numb to notice.

"Very good," said Queen Levana. "Thaumaturge Tavaler, see to it that the rest of the sentencing is duly carried out."

"Yes, My Queen."

Winter forced her eyes open. The ice had made its way up her throat now, was climbing over her jawline. There were tears freezing inside their ducts. There was saliva crystallizing on her tongue.

In the center of the room, a servant was cleaning the blood from the tiles. Aimery was rubbing his knife with a cloth. He met Winter's gaze and his smile was searing. "I am afraid the princess has no stomach for these proceedings."

The nobles in the audience tittered—Winter's disgust of the trials was a source of merriment to most of Levana's court.

She heard the rustle of her stepmother's gown as the queen turned to peer down at her, but Winter couldn't look up. She was a girl made of ice and glass. Her teeth were brittle, her lungs too easily shattered.

"Yes," said Levana. "I often forget she's here at all. You're about as useless as a rag doll, aren't you, Winter?"

The audience chuckled again, louder now, as if the queen had given permission to mock the young princess.

But Winter couldn't respond, not to the queen, not to the laughter. She kept her gaze pinned on the thaumaturge, trying to hide her panic.

"Oh no, she isn't quite as useless as that," Aimery said, still smiling. As Winter stared, a thin crimson line drew itself across his throat, blood bubbling up from the wound. "The prettiest girl on all of Luna? She will make some member of this court a very happy bride someday, I should think."

"The prettiest girl, Aimery?" Levana's light tone almost concealed the snarl beneath.

Aimery seamlessly slipped into a bow. "Prettiest only, My Queen. But no mortal could compare with your perfection."

The court was quick to agree, offering a hundred compliments at once, though Winter could still feel the leering gazes of more than one noble attached to her.

Aimery took a step toward the throne and his severed head tipped off, thunking against the marble and rolling, rolling, rolling, until it stopped right at Winter's frozen feet.

Still smiling.

She whimpered, but the sound was buried beneath the snow in her throat.

It's all in your head.

"Silence," said Levana, once she'd had her share of praise. "Are we finished?"

Finally, the ice found her eyes and Winter had no choice but to shut them against Aimery's headless apparition, enclosing herself in cold and darkness.

She would die here and not complain. She would be buried beneath this avalanche of lifelessness. She would never have to witness another murder again.

"There is one more prisoner still to be tried, My Queen." Aimery's voice echoed in the cold hollowness of Winter's head. "Sir Jacin Clay, royal guard, pilot, and assigned protector of Thaumaturge Sybil Mira."

Winter gasped and the ice shattered, a million sharp glittering bits exploding across the throne room and skidding across the floor. No one else heard them. No one else noticed.

Aimery, head very much attached, was watching her again, as if he'd been waiting to see her reaction. His smirk was subtle as he returned his attention to the queen.

"Ah, yes," said Levana. "Bring him in."

Two

THE DOORS TO THE THRONE ROOM OPENED, AND THERE he was, walking stiffly between two guards, his wrists corded behind his back. His blond hair was clumped and matted, strands of it clinging to his jaw. It appeared to have been a fair while since he'd last showered or enjoyed a full meal, but Winter could detect no obvious sign of abuse.

Her stomach flipped. All the heat that the ice had sucked out of her came rushing back to the surface of her skin.

Stay with me, Princess. Listen to my voice, Princess.

He was led to the center of the room, devoid of expression. Winter jabbed her fingernails into her palms.

Jacin didn't look at her. Not once.

"Jacin Clay," said Aimery, "you have been charged with betraying the crown by failing to protect Thaumaturge Mira, an action which ultimately resulted in her untimely death at the hands of the enemy, and also by failing to apprehend a known Lunar fugitive despite nearly two weeks spent in said fugitive's company. You are a traitor to Luna and to our queen. These crimes are punishable by death. What have you to say in your defense?"

Winter's heart thundered like a drum against her ribs. She tore her gaze from Jacin and looked pleadingly up at her stepmother, but Levana was not paying any attention to her.

"I plead guilty to all stated crimes," said Jacin, drawing Winter's attention back, "*except* for the accusation that I am a traitor."

Levana's fingernails fluttered against the arm of her throne. "Explain yourself."

Jacin stood as tall and stalwart as if he'd been in uniform, as if he were on duty, not on trial. "As I've said before, I did not apprehend the fugitive while in her company because I was attempting to convince her that I could be trusted, in order to gather information that I could later relay to my queen."

"Ah yes, you were spying on her and her friends," said Levana. "I do recall that excuse from when you were captured. I also recall that you had no pertinent information to give me, only lies."

"Not lies, My Queen, though I will admit that I underestimated the cyborg and her abilities. She was clearly disguising them from me."

"So much for earning her trust." There was mocking in the queen's tone.

"Knowledge of the cyborg's skills was not the only information I sought, My Queen."

"I suggest you stop playing with words, Sir Clay. My patience with you is already thin."

Winter's heart shriveled. Not Jacin. She could not sit here and watch them kill Jacin.

She would bargain for him, she decided, though the decision came with an obvious flaw. What did she have to bargain with? Nothing but her own life, and she knew Levana would not accept that.

Perhaps she could throw a fit. Go into hysterics. It would hardly be a stretch from the truth at this point, and it might distract them for a time, but she knew it would only delay the inevitable.

She had felt helpless so many times in her life, but never like this.

Only one thing to be done, then.

She would throw her own body in front of the blade.

Oh, Jacin would *hate* that.

Ignorant of Winter's newest resolve, Jacin respectfully

inclined his head. "During my time with Linh Cinder, I uncovered information about a device that can nullify the effects of the Lunar gift when connected to a person's nervous system."

This caused a curious squirm through the crowd. A stiffening of spines, a tilting forward of shoulders.

"Impossible," said Levana.

"Linh Cinder had evidence of its potential, My Queen. As it was described to me, on an Earthen, the device will keep their bioelectricity from being tampered with. But on a Lunar, it will prevent them from using their gift at all. Linh Cinder herself had the device installed when she arrived at the Commonwealth ball. Only when it was destroyed was she able to use her gift—as was evidenced with your own eyes, My Queen."

His words carried an air of impertinence and Winter noticed Levana's knuckles go white.

"How many of these hypothetical devices exist?"

"To my knowledge, only the broken device installed in the cyborg herself. But I suspect it would only require the patents and blueprints to make another. The inventor was Linh Cinder's adoptive father."

The queen's grip began to relax. "This is intriguing information, Sir Clay. But it speaks more of a desperate attempt to save yourself than true innocence."

Winter pressed her lips tight together.

"I agree, My Queen. But if my loyalty to the crown cannot be seen in how I conducted myself with the enemy, obtaining this information and alerting Thaumaturge Mira to the plot to kidnap Emperor Kaito, I don't know what other evidence I can provide for you, My Queen."

"Yes, yes, the anonymous tip that Sybil received, alerting her to Linh Cinder's plans." Levana sighed. "I find it very convenient that this comm you *claim* to have sent was seen by no one other than Sybil herself, who is now dead."

For the first time, Jacin looked off-balance beneath the queen's glare. He still had not looked at Winter.

The queen turned to her captain of the guard. "Jerrico, you were with Sybil when she ambushed the enemy's ship that day, and yet you said before that Sybil had mentioned no such comm. Have you anything to add?"

Jerrico took a step forward. He had returned from their Earthen excursion with a fair share of bruises on his face, but they had begun to fade. He fixed his eyes on Jacin. "My Queen, Thaumaturge Mira seemed confident that we would find Linh Cinder on that rooftop, but at the time, she did not mention receiving any outside information—anonymous or otherwise. When the ship landed, it was Thaumaturge Mira who ordered Jacin Clay to be taken into custody."

Jacin's eyebrow twitched. "Perhaps she was still upset

that I'd shot her." He paused, before adding, "While under Linh Cinder's control, in my defense."

"You seem to have plenty to say in your defense," said Levana.

Jacin didn't respond, just held her gaze with casual indifference. It was the calmest Winter had ever seen a prisoner in that room—he, who knew better than anyone the horrible things that happened on this floor, in the very spot where he stood. Levana should have been infuriated by his audacity, but she seemed merely thoughtful.

"Permission to speak, My Queen?"

The crowd rustled and it took a moment for Winter to discern who had spoken. It was a *guard*. One of the silent ornamentations of the palace. Though she recognized him, she did not know his name.

It took a moment for Levana to respond, and Winter could imagine her calculating whether to grant the permission, or punish the man for speaking out of turn. Finally, she nodded.

The guard stepped forward, staring at the wall, always at the wall. "My name is Liam Kinney, My Queen, and I was also a part of the team on the rooftop that day, along with Thaumaturge Mira."

A questioning eyebrow to Jerrico; a confirming nod received.

"As it was, I also assisted with the retrieval of

Thaumaturge Mira's body. We found her in possession of a portscreen. Though it was largely destroyed in the fall, it was nevertheless submitted as potential evidence in the case of her murder. I only wondered if anyone had attempted to retrieve the alleged comm."

Levana turned her attention back to Aimery, whose face was a mask that Winter recognized. The more pleasant his expression, the more annoyed he was. "In fact, our team did manage to access her recent communications," he said. "I was just about to bring forward the evidence."

It was a lie, and that gave Winter some hope. Aimery was a great liar, especially when it was in his best interests. And he *hated* Jacin, which meant he would not want to give up anything that could potentially save him.

Hope. Frail, flimsy, pathetic *hope.*

Aimery gestured toward the door and a servant scurried forward, carrying a shattered portscreen and a holograph node on a tray. "This is the portscreen that Sir Kinney mentioned. Our investigation has confirmed that there was, indeed, an anonymous comm sent to Sybil that morning."

"What did it say?" asked Levana.

Aimery nodded at the servant, who turned on the node. A holograph shimmered into the center of the room— behind it, Jacin faded away like a phantom.

The holograph displayed a basic text comm.

Linh Cinder to kidnap EC Emperor. Escape
planned from north tower rooftop at
sunset.

So much importance pressed into so few words. It was
just like Jacin.

Levana read the words with narrowed eyes. "Fascinat-
ing. Thank you, Sir Kinney, for bringing this to our attention."
It was telling that she did not thank Aimery, and Winter
shifted with embarrassment on his behalf, her own internal
pleasure barely surfacing amid the cloud of dread. Levana
continued, "I suppose you will tell me, Sir Clay, that this was
the comm you sent."

"It was, My Queen."

"Have you anything else to add before I make my
verdict?"

"Nothing, My Queen."

Levana slowly leaned back in her throne and the room
hushed, everyone breathlessly awaiting the queen's decision.

"I trust my stepdaughter would like me to spare you,"
said Levana.

Winter winced at the haughtiness in her tone. Jacin had
no reaction at all.

"Please, stepmother," she whispered, barely able to form

the words around her dry tongue. "It's *Jacin*. He is not our enemy."

"Not *yours*, perhaps," Levana said, her gaze ever pinned on the prisoner. "But you are a naïve, stupid girl."

"That is not so, My Queen. I am a factory for blood and platelets, and all my machinery is freezing over...."

The court burst into laughter, and Winter recoiled. Even Levana's lips twitched, though there was annoyance beneath the amusement.

"I have made my decision," she said, her booming voice demanding silence. "I have decided...to let the prisoner live."

Winter released a cry of relief. She clapped a hand over her mouth, but it was too late to stifle the noise.

There were more giggles from the audience, but Jacin's eyes stayed stoically glued to the queen.

"Have you any other insights to add, Princess?" Levana hissed through her teeth.

Winter gathered her emotions as well as she could. "No, My Queen. Your rulings are always wise and final, My Queen."

"This ruling is not finished." The queen's voice hardened as she addressed Jacin again. "Your inability to kill or capture Linh Cinder will not go unpunished, especially as your incompetence led to her successful kidnapping of my betrothed. For this crime, I sentence you to thirty self-inflicted lashings to be held on the central dais, followed by forty hours of penance. Your sentence shall commence at tomorrow's light-break."

Winter flinched, but even this punishment could not destroy the fluttery relief in her stomach. He was not going to die. She was not a girl of ice and glass at all, but a girl of sunshine and stardust, because Jacin wasn't going to die.

"And Winter . . ."

She jerked her attention back to her stepmother, who was eyeing her with disdain. "If you attempt to bring him food, I will have his tongue removed in payment for your kindness."

She shrank back into her chair, a tiny ray of the sunshine extinguished. "Yes, My Queen."

Three

WINTER WAS AWAKE HOURS BEFORE LIGHT BRIGHTENED
the dome's artificial sky, having hardly slept. She did not go
to watch Jacin receive his lashings on the city's central dais,
knowing that if he saw her, he would have kept himself from
screaming in pain. She wouldn't do that to him. Let him
scream. He was still stronger than any of them.

She dutifully nibbled at the cured meats and cheeses
that were brought in for her breakfast. She allowed the servants to bathe her and dress her in pale pink silk. She sat
through an entire session with Master Gertman, a third-tier
thaumaturge and her long-standing tutor, pretending to try
to use her gift and apologizing when it was too hard, when
she was too weak. He did not seem to mind anymore. He
spent most of their sessions gazing slack-jawed at her face,
and Winter didn't know if he would be able to tell if she
really did glamour him for once.

The day had fully come and gone, one of the maidservants had brought her a mug of warmed milk and cinnamon and turned down her bed, and finally Winter was left alone.

Her heart began to pound with anticipation.

She slipped into a pair of lightweight linen pants and a loose top, then pulled on her night robe so that it would look as if she were wearing her bedclothes underneath. She had thought of this all day, the plan forming slowly in her mind, like tiny puzzle pieces snapping together. Willful determination had kept any hallucinations at bay.

She fluffed her hair so that it might look like she'd woken from a deep slumber, turned off the lights, and climbed up onto her bed. The dangling chandelier clipped against her brow and she flinched, stepping back and catching her balance on the thick mattress.

Winter braced herself with a breath full of intentions.

Counted to three.

And screamed.

She screamed like an assassin was driving a knife into her stomach.

She screamed like a thousand birds were pecking at her flesh.

She screamed like the palace was burning down around her.

The guard stationed outside her door burst inside,

weapon drawn. Winter went on screaming. Stumbling back over her pillows, she pressed her back against the head-board and clawed at her hair.

"Princess! What is it? What's wrong?" His eyes darted wildly around the dark room, searching for an intruder, a threat.

Flailing an arm behind her, Winter scratched at the wallpaper, tearing off a shred. It was becoming easier to believe that she was truly horrified. There were phantoms and murderers closing in around her.

"Princess!" A second guard burst into the room. He must have heard her from down the hall. He flipped on the light and Winter ducked away from it. "What's going on?"

"I don't know." The first guard had crossed to the other side of the room and was checking behind the window drapes.

"*Monster!*" Winter shrieked, bulleting the statement with a sob. "I woke up and he was standing over my bed—one of—one of the queen's soldiers!"

The guards traded looks, and the silent message was clear, even to Winter.

Nothing's wrong. She's just crazy.

"Your Highness—" started the second guard as a third appeared at the doorway.

Good. There were usually only three guards stationed in this corridor, between her bedroom and the main stairway.

"He went that way!" Cowering behind one arm, Winter pointed toward the chambers that housed her washroom and dressing closet. "Please. Please don't let him get away. Please find him!"

"What's happened?" asked the newcomer.

"She thinks she saw one of the mutant soldiers," grumbled the second guard.

"*He was here!*" she screamed, so loud she felt the words tearing at her throat, but she pressed on. "Why aren't you protecting me? Why are you standing there? *Go find him!*"

The first guard looked sorely annoyed, as if this charade had interrupted something more than just standing in the hallway, staring at a wall. He holstered his gun, but said, with authority, "Of course, Princess. We will find this perpetrator and ensure your safety." He beckoned the second guard and the two of them stalked off toward the washroom.

Winter turned her pleading eyes on the third guard, falling into a crouch on the bed. "You must go with them," she urged, her voice fluttery and weak. "He is a monster—enormous—with gaping teeth and claws that will tear them to *shreds*. They can't defeat him alone, and if they fail—!" Her words turned into a wail of terror. "He'll come for me, and there will be no one to stop him. No one will save me!" She pulled at her hair, her entire body quivering.

"All right, all right. Of course, Highness. Just wait here,

and ... try to calm yourself." Looking grateful to leave the mad princess behind, he took off after his comrades.

No sooner had he disappeared through the open door did Winter slip off the bed and shrug out of her robe, leaving it draped over a chair.

"The closet is clear!" one of the guards yelled.

"Keep looking!" she yelled back. "I know he's in there!"

Snatching up the simple hat and shoes she'd left by the door, she fled.

Unlike her personal guards, who would have questioned her endlessly and insisted on escorting her into the city, the guards who were manning the towers outside the palace hardly stirred when she asked that the gate be opened for her departure. Without guards and fine dresses, and with her bushel of hair tucked up and her face tucked down, she could pass for a servant in the shadows.

As soon as she was outside the gate, she started to run again.

There were aristocrats milling around the tiled city streets, laughing and flirting in their fine clothes and glamours. Light spilled from open doorways, music danced along the window ledges, and everywhere was the smell of food and the clink of glasses and shadows kissing and sighing in darkened alleyways.

It was like this always in the city. The frivolity, the

pleasure. The white city of Artemisia—their own little paradise beneath the protective glass.

At the center of it all was the dais, a circular platform where dramas were performed and auctions held, where spectacles of illusion and bawdy humor often drew the families from their mansions for a night of revelry.

Public humiliations and punishments were frequently on the docket.

Winter was panting, both frazzled and giddy with her success, as the dais came into view. Then she saw him and the yearning inside her nearly buckled her knees. She had to slow to catch her breath.

He was sitting with his back to the enormous sundial that stood at the center of the dais, an instrument as useless as it was striking during these long nights. Ropes bound his bare arms and his chin was collapsed against his collarbone, his pale hair hiding his face. As Winter neared him, she could see the raised hatchmarks of the lashings across his chest and abdomen, scattered with dried blood. There would be more on his back. His hand would be blistered from gripping the lash. *Self-inflicted*, Levana had proclaimed the punishment, but everyone knew that Jacin would be under the control of a thaumaturge. There was nothing *self*-inflicted about it.

She wondered if Aimery had been the one to do it. He had probably volunteered, and relished in every wound.

Jacin raised his head as she reached the edge of the dais. Their eyes clashed, and for a moment, she was staring at a man who had been beaten and bound and mocked and tormented all day by passing onlookers, and for that one moment, she thought he must be broken. Just another one of the queen's broken toys.

But then one side of his mouth lifted, and the smile hit his startling blue eyes, and he was as bright and welcoming as the rising sun.

"Hey, Trouble," he said, leaning his head back against the dial.

With that, the terror from the past weeks slipped away as if they had never happened. He was alive. He was home. He was still Jacin.

She pulled herself onto the dais. "Do you have any idea how worried I've been?" she said, crossing to him. "I didn't know if you were dead or being held hostage, or if you'd been eaten by one of the queen's soldiers. It's been driving me mad not knowing."

He quirked an eyebrow at her.

She scowled. "Don't comment on that."

"I wouldn't dare." He rolled his shoulders as much as he could against his bindings. His wounds gapped and puckered with that slight movement, and his face contorted in pain, but it was brief.

Pretending she hadn't noticed, Winter sat cross-legged in front of him, inspecting the wounds. Wanting to touch him. Terrified to touch him. That much, at least, had not changed. "Does it hurt very much?"

"Better than being at the bottom of the lake." His smile turned wry, lips chapped from the harsh Earthen sun. "They'll move me to a suspension tank tomorrow night. Half a day and I'll be good as new." He squinted. "That's assuming you're not here to bring me food. I'd like to keep my tongue where it is, thank you."

"No food. Just a friendly face."

"Friendly." His gaze raked over her, his relaxed grin still in place. "That's an understatement."

She dipped her head, turning away just enough to hide the three scars that trailed down her right cheek. For years, Winter had assumed that when people stared at her, it was because the scars disgusted them. A rare disfigurement in their world of perfection. But then a maid had told her they weren't disgusted, they were in awe. She said the scars made Winter interesting to look at and somehow, odd as it was, even more beautiful. *Beautiful.* It was a word that Winter had heard tossed around all her life. A beautiful child, a beautiful girl, a beautiful young lady, so beautiful, *too* beautiful . . . and the stares that came with the word never ceased to make her want to don a veil like her stepmother's and hide from the whispers.

Jacin was the only person who could make her feel beautiful without it seeming like a bad thing. She couldn't recall him ever using the word, or making any such deliberate compliment. It was always hidden behind careless jokes that made her heart pound so fast.

"Don't tease," she said, flustered at the way he looked at her, at the way he always looked at her.

"Wasn't teasing," he said, all nonchalance.

In response, Winter reached out and punched him lightly on the shoulder—where there weren't any wounds.

He flinched, and she gasped—ready to apologize—but his eyes stayed warm. "That's not a fair fight, Princess."

She reeled back the apology. "It's about time I had the advantage."

He looked past her, into the streets. "Where's your guard?"

"I left him behind. Searching for a monster in my closet."

With that, the sunshine smile was gone, hardened into exasperation. "Princess, you can't go out alone. If something happened to you—"

"Who's going to hurt me here, in the city? Everyone knows who I am."

"It just takes one idiot, too used to getting what he wants and too drunk to control himself."

Flushing, she clenched her jaw.

Jacin looked immediately regretful. "Princess—"

"I'll run all the way back to the palace. I'll be fine."

He sighed, and she listed her head, wishing she'd brought some sort of medicinal salve for his cuts. Levana hadn't said anything about medicine, and the sight of him tied up and vulnerable—and shirtless, even if it was a bloodied shirtless—was making her fingers twitch in odd ways.

"I just wanted to be alone with you," she said, focusing on his face. "We never get to be alone anymore."

"It's not proper for seventeen-year-old princesses to be alone with young men who have questionable intentions."

She laughed. "And what about young men who she's been best friends with since she was barely old enough to walk?"

He shook his head. "Those are the worst."

She snorted—an actual snort of laughter that served to brighten Jacin's smile again.

But the humor was bittersweet. The truth was, Jacin only touched her when he was helping her through a particularly awful hallucination. Otherwise, he hadn't deliberately touched her in years. Not since she was fourteen and he was sixteen and she'd tried to teach him the Eclipse Waltz with somewhat embarrassing results.

These days, she would have auctioned off the Milky Way to make his intentions a little less honorable.

Her smile started to fizzle, and then his did too. "I've missed you," she said.

His gaze dropped away and he shifted in an attempt to get more comfortable against the dial. Locking his jaw so she wouldn't see how much every tiny movement pained him. "How's your head?" he asked, once her words had cloaked them both.

"The visions come and go," she said, "but they don't seem to be getting worse."

"Have you had one today?"

She picked at a small, natural flaw in the linen of her pants, thinking back. "No, not since the trials yesterday. I turned into a girl of icicles, and Aimery lost his head. Literally."

"Wouldn't mind so much if that last one came true."

She shushed him.

"I mean it. I don't like how he looks at you these days."

Winter glanced over her shoulder, but the courtyards surrounding the dais were empty. Only the distant bustle of music and laughter reminded her that they were in a metropolis at all.

"You're back on Luna now," she said. "You have to be careful what you say."

"You're giving *me* advice on how to be covert?"

"Jacin—"

"There are three cameras on this square. Two on the lampposts behind you, one embedded in the oak tree behind the sundial. None of them have audio. Unless she's hiring lip-readers now?"

Winter scowled. "How can you know that for sure?"

"Surveillance was one of Sybil's specialties."

Winter crossed her arms. "She could have killed you yesterday. You need to be careful."

"I know, Princess. I have no interest in returning to that throne room as anything other than a loyal guard."

A burst of lights overhead caught Winter's eye and she glanced up. Through the dome, the flames of a dozen spaceships were already fading as they launched themselves from Luna's ports and streaked across the star-scattered sky. Heading toward Earth.

"Soldiers," said Jacin, following her gaze. She couldn't tell if he'd meant it as a statement or a question. "How's the war effort?"

"No one tells me anything. But Her Majesty seems pleased with our victories so far . . . though still furious about the missing emperor, and the canceled wedding."

"Not canceled. Just delayed."

"Try telling her that."

He grunted.

Winter leaned forward on her elbows, cupping her chin. "Did the cyborg really have a device like you talked about at the trial? One that can keep people from being manipulated?"

A light sparked in his eyes, as if she'd reminded him of something important, but when he tried to lean toward her, his binds held him back. He grimaced and cursed beneath his breath.

Winter scooted closer to him, making up the distance herself.

"That's not all," he said. "Supposedly, this device can keep Lunars from using their gift in the first place."

"Yes, you mentioned that in the throne room."

His gaze burrowed into her. "*And* it will protect their minds. She said it keeps them from . . ."

Going crazy.

He didn't have to say it out loud, not when his eyes had so much hope and so much sympathy and when he was looking at her like he'd finally solved the world's greatest problem. His meaning hung between them.

A device like that could heal her.

Winter's fingers curled up and settled under her chin. "You said there weren't any more of them."

"No. But if we could find the patents for the invention . . . to even know it's possible . . ."

"Now that the queen knows, she'll do anything to keep more from being made."

His expression darkened, his body slumped. "I know, but I had to offer something. If only Sybil hadn't arrested me in the first place, ungrateful witch." Winter smiled gently, and when Jacin caught the look, his irritation melted away. "Doesn't matter. Now I know it's possible, I'll find a way to do it."

"The visions are never so bad when you're around. They'll be better now that you're back."

She thought he flinched, but maybe it was the flicker of torches around the dais.

"I'm sorry I left," he said. "I regretted it as soon as I realized what I'd done. It happened so fast, and then I couldn't come back for you. I'd just ... abandoned you up here. With her. With *them*."

"You didn't abandon me. You were taken hostage. You didn't have a choice."

His brow furrowed and, after a moment, he met her eyes again. This time, there was truth in the look.

She straightened. "You weren't manipulated?"

"Not the whole time," he whispered, like a confession. "I chose to side with them, when Sybil and I boarded their ship." Guilt washed over his face, and it was such an odd expression on him Winter wasn't sure she was interpreting it right. "Then, I betrayed them." He leaned his head back against the sundial again, harder than necessary. "You should hate me. I'm an idiot. I made a mistake."

"You may be an idiot, but I assure you, you're quite a lovable one."

He shook his head. "You're the only person in the galaxy who would ever call me *lovable*."

"I'm the only person in the galaxy crazy enough to believe it. Now tell me what happened. What mistake did you make that is worth hating you for?"

He swallowed, hard. "That cyborg Her Majesty wants to find so much?"

"Linh Cinder."

"Yeah. Well, I thought she was just some crazy girl on a suicide mission, right? I figured she was going to get us all killed with these delusions of kidnapping the emperor and overthrowing the queen . . . to listen to her talk, anyone would have thought that. So I figured, I'd rather take a chance and come back to you, if I could. Let her throw her own life away."

"But Linh Cinder did kidnap the emperor. And she got away."

"I know." He shifted his attention back to Winter. "Sybil took one of her friends hostage, a redhead girl. Don't suppose you know—"

Winter beamed. "Oh, yes. Her name is Scarlet. The queen gave her to me as a pet, and she's being kept in the menagerie. I like her a great deal." Her brow creased. "Although I can't tell if she's decided to like me or not."

He flinched at a sudden unknown pain and spent a moment re-situating himself. "Can you get her a message for me?"

"Of course."

"You have to be careful. I won't tell you if you can't be discreet—for your own sake."

"I can be discreet."

Jacin looked skeptical.

"I *can*. I will be as secretive as a spy. As secretive as *you*."

Jacin set his jaw and Winter scooted in just a bit closer. His voice fell, as if he were no longer so certain those cameras didn't come with audio. "Tell her they're coming for her."

Winter stared. "Coming for . . . coming here?"

He nodded, a subtle dip of his head. "And I think they might actually have a chance."

Frowning, Winter reached forward and tucked the strands of Jacin's sweat- and dirt-stained hair behind his ears. He tensed at the touch, but didn't pull away. "Jacin Clay," she said softly, "you're speaking in riddles."

"Linh Cinder." His voice became hardly more than a

breath, and she tilted closer yet to hear him. A curl of her hair fell against his shoulder. He licked his lips. "She's Selene."

Every muscle in her body tightened. She pulled back. "Jacin. If Her Majesty heard you say—"

"I won't tell anyone else. But I had to tell you." His eyes crinkled at the corners, full of sympathy. "I know you loved her."

Her heart thumped. "My Selene?"

"Yes. But . . . I'm sorry, Princess. I don't think she remembers you."

Winter blinked, letting the daydream fill her up for one hazy moment. Selene, alive. Her cousin, her friend. *Alive.*

But then she shook her head, casting the hope away and scrunching her shoulders against her neck. "No. She's dead. I was *there,* Jacin. I saw the aftermath of the fire."

"You didn't see *her.*"

"They found—"

"Charred flesh. I know."

"A pile of girl-shaped ashes."

"They were just ashes. Look, I didn't believe it either, but I do now." One corner of his mouth tilted up, into something like pride. "She's our lost princess. And she's coming home."

A throat cleared behind Winter, and her skeleton nearly leaped from her skin. She swiveled her torso around, falling onto her elbow in the process.

Her personal guard was standing just off the dais, wearing a dark scowl.

"Ah!" Heart fluttering with a thousand startled birds, Winter broke into a relieved smile. "Did you catch the monster?"

There was no return smile, not even a flush of his cheeks, which was the normal reaction when she let loose that particular smile. Instead, her guard seemed to be developing a twitch over his right eye.

"Your Highness. I have come to retrieve you and escort you safely back to the palace."

Righting herself, Winter clasped her hands graciously in front of her chest. "Of course. It's so kind of you to worry after me." She glanced back at Jacin, who was eyeing the guard with distrust. No surprise. He eyed everyone with distrust. "I fear tomorrow will be even more difficult for you, Sir Clay. Do try to think of me when you can."

"*Try*, Princess?" He smirked, meeting her gaze again. "I can't seem to think of much else."

Thank you for reading this FEIWEL AND FRIENDS book.
The Friends who made

possible are:

Jean Feiwel
publisher

Liz Szabla
editor in chief

Rich Deas
senior creative director

Holly West
associate editor

Dave Barrett
executive managing editor

Nicole Liebowitz Moulaison
production manager

Lauren A. Burniac
editor

Anna Roberto
associate editor

Christine Barcellona
administrative assistant

Follow us on Facebook or visit us online at mackids.com.

OUR BOOKS ARE FRIENDS FOR LIFE